Praise

for A VENGEFUL SPIRIT

"Murder, mystery, mayhem are all found in Lizzy Armentrout's first novel A Vengeful Spirit (Shelly Gale Mystery)" —Keiki Hendrix

"...Clues and a potential romance will keep readers guessing in this highly accessible, straight-forward mystery. —B. Lynn Goodwin

"Really enjoyed this Christian cozy mystery, and especially loved hearing familiar names and places of rural NC and WV. —Bonnie Lambert

"...perfect balance between all things Christian and Murder Mystery...." —Christian Murder Mystery

"...The action was fast-paced and there were enough twists and turns to keep me guessing..." —Christian Mystery

SHELLY GALE MYSTERY SERIES

A Vengeful Spirit
A Covetous Spirit

Author, Lizzy Armentrout

LizzyArmentrout.com

A Shelly Gale Mystery
BOOK 2

LIZZY ARMENTROUT

A COVETOUS SPIRIT

WELCOME
ON BOARD

FSP
FIRST STEPS PUBLISHING
For the Author Seeking a Solid Foundation

First Steps Publishing
www.FirstStepsPublishing.com
ISBN: 978-1-944072-12-4 (pocketbook)

This novel is a work of fiction. Names, descriptions, entities, and incidents included in the story are products of the author's imagination. Any resemblance to actual persons, events, and entities, living or dead, is entirely coincidental.

Every effort has been made to be accurate. The author assumes no responsibility or liability for errors made in this book. The opinions expressed by the author are not necessarily those of First Steps Publishing.

Scriptures quotations used in this book are from the HOLY BIBLE, NEW INTERNATIONAL VERSION. Copyright © 1973, 1978, 1984 International Bible Society. Used by permission of Zondervan Bible Publishers or from the NEW AMERICAN STANDARD BIBLE®, Copyright © 1960, 1962, 1963, 1968, 1971, 1972, 1973, 1975, 1977, 1995 by The Lockman Foundation. Used by permission.

Images:
Hooded beach chairs on deck of a cruise ship; ©VanderWolf Images; Adobe Stock
Life Preserver; ©Oleg Lopatkin; Shutterstock.com

Originally published in hardcover by First Steps Publishing.
First mass market edition: May 2020

10 9 8 7 6 5 4 3 2
Printed in the United States of America

I dedicate this book to my
fabulous husband.
Todd has encouraged me to keep on
writing and
has been an excellent sounding
board for plot ideas.

Next to my salvation,
marrying him, my best friend,
was the best decision I ever made.
This book would not be possible
without him.

You have my love forever, Todd!

In Gratitude

So many have helped me through this second book. First, my two sounding boards for plot—Todd and David—thank you for all of your ideas, input, and critiques.

Secondly, my "reading group" on Facebook that did read-throughs to spot inconsistencies and grammatical problems. You all did a fantastic job, and this book wouldn't be a reality without your input. I hope you enjoy the final product!

Lastly, I thank the readers of book one for encouraging me to write this second book and for urging me on to finish. I hope you all fall in love with all of these characters as I have!

Chapter 1

Shelly stood at the front door of the church, looked around, and thanked the Lord for blessing them with such a beautiful day for a wedding. Even though it was mid-July, the humidity was low, and the temperature was in the low eighties. The beautiful Carolina blue sky was filled with tiny, fluffy white clouds resembling cotton balls. She couldn't have arranged for a more perfect day; God had truly blessed. *Thank you, Jesus, for sending us such perfect weather. I ask, if it be possible, that You help the rest of the day to go as beautifully as the weather.*

There were still many things to be completed before the big event, so Shelly roused herself and took off for the church's bridal room where the rest of the ladies were changing. When she opened the door, she had to smile at the contrast to the scene she had just left. Outside the church, everything was peaceful and lovely; inside the bridal room, everything was in a state of chaos—clothes were strewn everywhere, ladies and the flower girl were running around trying to find their dresses, shoes, flowers, makeup, etc.

"Shell, get in here and get going! Girl, where have you been? Here I am, a nervous wreck, waiting on you to help me, and you pick today to be late! You're never late!" Nicole demanded as she tugged Shelly over to her personal chaos in one of the corners.

"Oh, Nicole, take a chill pill. I'm only ten minutes late. Tim sent me on a special errand, and it took longer than I expected. But no worries, I'm here now, so let's get this show going."

"Tim? You saw Tim? Is he here? How does he look? Is he ready for the guys' pictures?"

"Nicole! Settle down and breathe. Yes, he's here, and I must say he looks quite handsome in his tux. And yes, the guys are already getting their pictures taken. Now we have forty-five minutes to make you so beautiful that Tim will have a heart attack when he sees you. No more chattering, let's get to work."

The forty-five minutes flew by as Shelly helped Nicole arrange her hair, veil, and makeup. The finishing touch was to put on her dress and shoes. After they finished, Nicole's father came in to have some pictures taken with the bride. He had been diagnosed with Alzheimer's disease a few months back, and it had advanced to the point that he was beginning to forget his family members, but when he stepped into the room and saw Nicole in her wedding dress, he stopped and said, with tears streaming down his face, "Look at my baby! Nicole, you look so beautiful and just like your mama on our wedding day. I sure do wish she could see you!" And when he raised her veil and kissed her on the cheek, Shelly looked around and noticed that there wasn't a dry eye in the room. *I'm so glad he's having one of his good days today! I hope he can stay in this frame of mind until the ceremony ends. Nicole would be so relieved.*

The wedding director came in and told them it was time to head upstairs. Shelly helped Nicole and her father up the steps to the front of the church. Once they were in place, Shelly once again sent a quick prayer to heaven asking for everything to go well. Then it was her turn to walk down the aisle. She was impressed with how beautifully the church was decorated. The ladies in Nicole's Sunday school class had volunteered to decorate for her, and they had done a marvelous job. There were blue, pink, yellow, and purple flower arrangements everywhere to match the bridesmaid's pastel dresses. At the front of the church stood a very nervous Tim with the pastor, and beside him stood Curly. She had to smile when he winked at her. They had been dating ever since returning from West Virginia four months earlier, but because each of them had such hectic schedules, many of their dates had fallen through. While Nicole and Tim had flown through their courtship, she and Curly planned on taking a much slower approach to their relationship.

Shelly found her marked spot and turned to watch Tucker, bursting with pride in his tuxedo and ring pillow, lead the procession down the aisle. She had to smile at the huge grin on Nicole's face. Nicole's eyes never once left Tim's face, even though she had to walk slowly to accommodate her father's shuffle. Mr. Sheldon proudly escorted his daughter to the front, and even remembered his line as he gave his daughter to Tim. After he returned to his seat at the front, Shelly breathed a huge sigh of relief. She and Nicole had spent many nights discussing whether or not he would be capable of giving Nicole away, but Nicole had decided that even if he had a bad day, her dad would have been devastated to be left out. Shelly was thankful that he had remained coherent and capable of doing his part to make Nicole's day special.

As the ceremony progressed, Shelly found herself looking at Curly, who looked so handsome in his black suit. She started daydreaming that it was their wedding and not Nicole's until one of the other bridesmaids had to nudge her to remind her to give Nicole Tim's ring.

The ceremony and pictures were finally over, and it was time for the reception. Since Nicole didn't make a huge income as a second grade Christian school teacher, several of the parents of her students had volunteered to make the food for her. It turned out better than if she had hired a catering company. It was finally time for Nicole to throw the bouquet and Tim to throw the garter. Shelly helped round up all the single men and had to laugh as Curly dove in front of everyone to catch it. When the time came for the bouquet to be thrown, Shelly was distracted by a crying baby, but after bouncing off several different ladies' hands, the bouquet landed right at her feet! While she and Curly were having their picture taken, she blushed when Curly whispered in her ear, "I think God is showing *us* something, Shell!"

The limo arrived, but before she could let them leave on their honeymoon, Shelly had one final job to do. She grabbed the microphone and asked for everyone's attention. Once everyone was quiet, she said, "Nicole, earlier you fussed at me for being ten minutes late, and I told you that I was late because Tim sent me on a special errand. Well, I need to apologize to both of you because I was really running an errand for you and Tim. You see, we knew that you had planned a simple three-day honeymoon in Gatlinburg, Tennessee, because we all know you are saving up to buy a house. However, Tim's dad thought, and I agreed, that we wanted to send you on a seven- day cruise to the Caribbean and Mexico! Tim, your father generously paid for the entire cruise, and for all the other expenses, your friends and coworkers generously chipped in as our wedding gift to you two. I was late because I was getting your summer clothes."

Shelly had to stop because Nicole started shrieking and crying. Nicole then hugged Shelly and Curly and thanked everyone for being such good friends. "Nicole, you need to hurry. You and Tim go change into some comfortable clothes, and your limo will be waiting at the front. The limo driver is going to stop by both of your places so you can pick up your passports. Hurry so you don't miss your plane!"

After the newlyweds had changed and run through the bird seed, Shelly ran up as they were getting into the limo and gave Nicole one last long hug. "Go and have a wonderful time! No one deserves it more than you two."

As Shelly and Curly watched the limo pull out with the newlyweds, they had no idea what they had just gotten their friends into.

Chapter 2

Nicole and Tim spent the ride to the airport on cloud nine as they looked through their packets of information about their upcoming cruise. They could not get over the generosity of their friends and family and could not wait to see the ship since neither of them had ever been on a cruise. Their packet had everything they needed—an itinerary, paid excursions at every port, spending money, cabin assignments, ship information, and brochures for the countries to which they would be sailing.

"Tim, look at all of this! We're going to Cozumel, Costa Maya, Belize, and Nassau! I can't believe this. I'm so excited! Oh no! I didn't pack my camera. We'll have to ask the driver to stop at a drugstore so I can buy one."

"No problem, Nicky. You know Shelly, she thought of everything. As we were waiting for the limo to pull up, she told me that Curly had tucked our cell phones into my carry-on, so let's just use those for our photos. This is going to be a wonderful start to a wonderful marriage. I'm so thankful that God brought us together." Tim then drew her into his arms for a hug and a kiss.

The limo finally arrived at the Piedmont Triad International Airport in Greensboro, North Carolina, and they quickly checked their luggage and entered the dreaded line for security clearance. When it was finally their turn to go through the metal detector, Nicole breezed right through, but when Tim went through, the alarms went off. He sheepishly emptied his pockets, took off his belt, and handed them to the security officer. He stepped through again, and again the alarms went off. A security officer came and pulled him off to the side; he then used a black wand and waved it all over Tim's arms and legs. The wand's alarms went off too! The security officer then patted him down, and when he could not find anything, he called a senior officer over for assistance. By this time, Tim and Nicole were both growing embarrassed at all the attention he was receiving.

"Sir, by any chance, would you have had any surgeries where a piece of metal was placed inside your body?" the officer inquired.

"Let me think...oh yeah, I had my right leg shattered in a car wreck when I was a teenager, and the doctor had to put a steel rod into my leg. It's been so long ago that I'd almost forgotten about it. Could that be causing all of this trouble?"

"Yes, sir. That would do it. Since we didn't find anything when the other officer frisked you, I'm going to release you. Sorry for any inconvenience."

"Thank you, Officer. Nicky, we're going to have to hustle if we're gonna make it to our gate in time."

Nicole was thankful that they were flying out of Greensboro. Since it was a relatively small airport compared to either of the ones in Raleigh or Charlotte, they didn't have far to run. They just made it to the gate in time. When they finally found their seats, they breathed a huge sigh of relief that they hadn't missed their flight to Orlando. They spent the flight holding hands and dreaming about their future as husband and wife. When they exited the plane, they saw a man holding a sign that read, "Mr. & Mrs. Beaufort."

Tim strolled over to the man and discovered that a shuttle van had been arranged to take them to their departure port. Once they had claimed their luggage and were on their way, Nicole looked over at Tim, laughed, and said, "I had no idea our first day as husband and wife would be so hectic. It seems like all we've done so far is go from one line to another."

"I agree, but once we're on that ship and see those blue waters like we saw in those brochures, we'll be so glad that we didn't go to Gatlinburg. I wonder if we'll feel the ship moving and if we'll have a balcony. By the way, do you get motion sickness?"

"No, not that I know of. How 'bout you?"

"Me either. That's good. I would hate to have you sick the whole week."

The shuttle finally reached the Port Canaveral loading area for the ship. They could not believe the number of vehicles that were in line and how long it took just to get to the unloading area. After a twenty- minute wait, the shuttle reached the drop-off area. While they were unloading their luggage, a cruise ship employee came by and tagged their luggage with their cabin number; he then threw all their luggage into a huge trailer to be taken to the ship. He pointed them to a line that was forming on the sidewalk, so they headed over there to wait once again, to show their identification and passports to the lady at the door.

As they stood waiting out in the hot Florida sun, they had to smile at the parents trying to console their fussy children. Then Nicole overheard a couple behind them talking about their wedding.

Nicole turned and asked, "Are you newlyweds too?"

Giggling, the young lady answered, "Yes, how did you know?"

"Um, I could just tell. Is this your first cruise?"

"Oh, yes! We're from New York and can't wait to see the blue waters and feel the hot sun."

"Mitsi, please. You don't need to bother these people with our life history. Why don't you just leave them alone?" Her husband interrupted.

"Oh, excuse me then," Nicole replied, turned to Tim, shrugged her shoulders, and raised her eyebrows at him.

Tim leaned in close and whispered, "Doesn't sound like a happy newlywed couple, does it? Wonder what the husband's problem is." Nicole just giggled and shrugged. Before they knew it, it was their turn to juggle their carry-ons and show their passports and identifications.

When they were cleared, they entered the door and discovered another metal detector. "Oh, great! Here we go again," Tim grunted. Hoping to prevent another drawn-out scene, he told the security officer about the rod in his leg. So, Nicole breezed through the detector, and Tim went through another frisking. After successfully passing through security, they followed the people in front of them up the escalator. At the top, they entered a huge room with high ceilings and people everywhere.

"Honey, do you have any idea what we do next?" Nicole asked.

"Well, I know I want you to hold onto my hand. I sure don't want to lose my wife in this crowd when I just got you. It looks like they've got the room divided into two lines." Tim was interrupted by a cruise official who pointed them to a tall table to fill out their custom's forms. The official then told them that after filling out the forms, they were to enter the line according to their last name.

Tim took care of the paperwork, while Nicole took their carry-ons and tried to get out of the way. When he was finished, he helped Nicole with their stuff and found the line for their last name ending in B.

"Can you believe all of this? I never knew people went through so much just to go on a vacation," he told Nicole while standing in line.

"I know. This is crazy, honey. What do you think about that couple we met in line? Something's weird there. While you were filling out the custom's forms,

I saw him fussing at her for dropping his carry-on. Doesn't sound like love to me."

"It's strange, I agree. Maybe we can meet them on the ship and get a chance to witness to them. Their relationship is not starting off well. Makes me thankful I've got you." Tim demonstrated his point with a quick kiss. Once they went through the line, they were directed to a cruise official at a counter. There they were given their cabin key card and soft drink cards, which they were delighted to discover were already paid for. They were then told that a thousand dollars had been deposited in an account for any charges they would incur while on the ship. As they struggled to overcome their surprise at the generous amount, the officer handed them more paperwork and pointed them to yet another door. When they stepped through that door, they saw the ship for the first time.

Tim nudged Nicole and said with awe in his voice, "That ship is huge! Wow! It must be at least as tall as a ten-story building. Now that I see our ship, I'm getting really excited. We're gonna have the best honeymoon ever!"

They walked across the gangplank and entered through the side of the ship. When they stepped through the entrance, they found themselves in an extremely noisy lobby with some people eating, kids running around, piano music playing, and just general organized chaos. The captain welcomed them aboard, and another officer asked for their key cards and told them to stand still for a picture. When he handed their key cards back, he told them it had their photo embedded in it. The official explained they would need their card every time they left the ship and also when they reboarded at the different ports. He went on to explain that they were to use the card, and not cash, for all purchases onboard the ship. He then directed them to the elevators at the side of the lobby that would take them up to their deck. They took a moment to look around the grand lobby, which looked like an atrium. It had ceilings nine decks high, and different colored lights were shining on the walls. In the middle of the room was a piano with someone playing soft classical music. Off to one side was a large spiral staircase leading to another deck. The glass elevators were to the right of the piano, so Nicole and Tim made their way to them.

After they got off the elevators, Nicole and Tim felt like they were in a scavenger hunt. It took them forever to find cabin 7230 on the Empress Deck. As they finally approached their cabin, they heard raised voices from behind them. When they turned to look, they found it was that same couple entering a cabin five doors down from theirs, and they were arguing once again.

"Man, they need some serious help. Well, enough of the negative. I have a job to do. Here, let me have your things, honey." After taking Nicole's carry-on, Tim swept a giggling Nicole up into his arms and carried her across the threshold into their cabin. "Welcome to your first home as Mrs. Tim Beaufort, Nicky."

"Oh, Tim, you're such a romantic. I love you!" After sharing a kiss, Tim set her down, and they explored their cabin. They were delighted to discover that they did indeed have a balcony, and on the desk they discovered a note saying:

> *Enjoy your new lives together as*
> *Mr. & Mrs. Beaufort.*
>
> *Love,*
> *Your friends & family*

Chapter 3

Nicole and Tim had just started to explore their cabin when there was a knock on their door.

"Wonder who that could be." Tim said as Nicole shrugged in response. When he opened the door, a steward stepped in and introduced himself as Alfonso and that he was from the country of Spain; he explained that the employees on ship came from various countries around the world. When he discovered that this was their first cruise, he explained to them about their dinnertime and seating assignments for the formal dining room being on their key cards. He also explained that the expected attire for dinner did not have to be formal but that it was to be, at least, business casual with no shorts or tank tops permitted in the formal dining room. If they didn't wish to dress for dinner, they could eat at the buffet or the grill. Alfonso went on to say that he would be their steward for the whole cruise and would be happy to help in any way. As he was finishing his welcome aboard speech, he was interrupted by an announcement on the hallway intercom from Big Al, the ship's activity director, announcing that the safety drill would begin in ten minutes.

After Big Al finished, Alfonso showed them their life vests hidden away under the closet and gave them directions to the section of the main deck that they were to report to.

When they stepped out into the hallway, they realized they did not need to worry about getting lost. They just entered the mass of people already making their way to the stairwell. At each landing of the stairwell, there was an official shouting out directions about where they were to go. Nicole and Tim just followed the rest of the people out onto the main deck and lined up according to the instructions being given over the intercom. Tim reached over, drew Nicole close, and whispered in her ear, "Check out who's in our line at the end." Nicole couldn't believe it when she looked and saw the couple they had seen arguing all day. The man and woman were both standing in their line, but they weren't touching or talking, just glumly staring straight ahead.

"I can't believe that on such a huge ship as this we keep bumping into the same unhappy couple. I can just hear what Shelly would say if she were here. She'd tell me that God must be putting them in my path for a purpose, and I must say I'd have to agree. I've never seen a more miserable couple, especially for newlyweds. Tim, we're gonna have to pray and ask God for direction on how to approach them so that we can share His love with them."

"I agree totally, hon. Oh, they're starting. We'd better listen." The safety drill seemed like it went on for hours, but twenty minutes later, they were following the crowd back the way they had come. As Tim was leading Nicole back up the stairwell, someone bumped into him. When he turned to look, he was shocked to see that it was Barry and Janet Schmidt from back home.

"Barry? Janet? What on earth, I can't believe this! Nicky, this is Barry and Janet Schmidt. They're from King too. Barry and Janet, I'd like to introduce you to my new wife, Nicole."

"Gotcha a wife, huh? Ya mean there's someone who loves ya? Just joking, man! I can't believe we ran into someone we know all the way down here in Florida on this monster cruise ship and that we'd run into you of all people. Janet, ain't this just something? Wait'll we tell the kids!" Barry shouted.

"Where are your two boys? I don't see them anywhere," Tim asked as he looked around at all the people going back to their cabins.

"Them two? Aw, they're home with their granny. You 'member her? I wanted us a vacation, and there's no way we'd have gotten one with those two brats along," Barry answered.

"Barry! Behave!" Janet reprimanded.

"Shucks, hon, you know it's the God's-honest truth!"

"Well, we won't keep you, and we hope you get the vacation you're hoping for," Tim said as he shook their hands.

As they continued their trek back to their cabin, Nicole commented, "Well, they seemed like such a lovely couple, I guess. How do you know them?"

"Nice. Huh! Not one bit! That is one messed-up family, and they don't like me even one little bit. I had to remove their two boys, a five-year-old and a seven- year-old, from their home a few months back after we discovered that the boys were being neglected. It wasn't mild neglect either. Their sons were scrounging in the neighbor's trash cans every day just to get something to eat. Their case is probably the worst case of neglect that I've seen so far as a social worker for the county. Anyway, when we removed the two boys, both parents went nutso on me. They have made my life very frustrating at DSS. Constant complaints, hateful phone calls, anything they can think of to harass me."

"How awful! And they seemed so nice too. Well, you know what they say is true. 'You can't judge a book by its cover.' Well, just forget about them. Hopefully we won't run into them anymore."

They had finally made it through the mob of people back to their cabin, and Tim responded as he closed the door behind him, "I'll be glad to forget them. I just want to focus on you right now anyway. I've been waiting my whole life for my wedding night, and you're all I've thought about for months now. Nicky, honey, have I told you how much I love you? I love your obvious love for God, your bubbling personality, your bright blue eyes that change shades whenever your mood changes, and your beautiful long blond hair. I even love how you're time-challenged and get so caught up in whatever is going on that you forget anyone or anything else. You've brought me so much joy in such a short amount of time, and I'm so thankful you agreed to be my wife."

"Oh, Tim, you're so sweet..." Nicole had planned on saying more, but her husband had other plans and interrupted her with a kiss.

***

The next morning, the newlyweds ordered room service for their late breakfast, and when it arrived, they took it out to the balcony so they could enjoy the magnificent scenery as they ate.

"Isn't this just the most beautiful thing you've ever seen?" Nicole asked with awe.

"Yes, it is," Tim replied, but when Nicole looked over at him, he was gazing at her.

"Tim! Stop! You're making me blush. I was talking about the ocean! Oh! Look, quick, look! See them?"

"What? What did you see?" Tim asked as he stood up and went to lean over the balcony.

"Look right over there and just keep on looking. There were dolphins jumping out of the ocean just a minute ago. Oh, there they are again! Did you see them?"

"Yes, they're amazing! What a beautiful sight! I've seen dolphins at Sea World before, but to see them in their natural habitat is just breathtaking."

"Oh, Tim, I can tell that this is just the beginning of a marvelous and wonderful honeymoon!" Nicole said as she wrapped her arm around her husband's shoulder and watched the dolphins racing the ship.

Nicole would later remember those words and that moment, and she would shake her head. They were in for a unique and adventurous honeymoon maybe, but their honeymoon would not turn out to be wonderful and marvelous.

Chapter 4

They spent most of the day exploring the ship from the topmost Sky Deck all the way down to the Riviera Deck, which was as far as they were permitted to go. They couldn't believe the variety of activities they discovered. Just on the Sun and Sky Decks, they found a jogging path, basketball and volleyball courts (of course, there were nets enclosing the area so balls wouldn't get lost at sea), a children's play world, and a small children's pool! They were delighted to discover the Serenity Area, which had many upscale loungers and big hammocks that were limited to just adult use so they could escape all the noise from the children's area. They decided they would have to come back and spend some time on the hammock reading a book while feeling the breeze from the ocean. The Lobby and Main Decks were their favorite decks due to the many shopping boutiques and the live piano music. When they made it to the Lido Deck, they discovered the main swimming pool and water slide. They were also thrilled to find a twenty-four-hour pizzeria, grill, and ice cream machine! Nicole had to laugh as Tim insisted on making her an ice cream cone which fell over when he handed it to her due to the heat. They were thankful to see drink stations at every corner since the weather was so hot and humid.

When they had finished their exploring, they decided they wanted to go back to their cabin and enjoy a nap. They had meant to just sleep an hour or two, but the gentle swaying of the ship kept them asleep for four hours. They had to rush to get dressed in order to make it to the formal dining room in time for their meal.

They had no idea what to expect when they entered the dining room, and Nicole could not take her eyes off all the beautiful decorations and the waiters standing at attention along the walls with white towels draped over their arms. The immaculately dressed maître d' checked their key cards and pointed them to their table.

Before Tim was even to the table, a waiter had pulled Nicole's chair out for her and seated her, even putting her napkin across her lap for her. "Allow me to introduce myself. I'm Ramone from the country of Honduras. I'll be your waiter every night of this cruise. My desire is to make your evening meals as pleasurable as possible. If you have a need, however small or large, please don't hesitate to ask. What may I get you to drink this evening?"

Ramone returned a few minutes later, and Nicole and Tim enjoyed watching him go through the same spiel for every couple that came to their table. There were eight place settings, and all but two had been filled when Ramone started taking their meal orders. As Tim was ordering his filet mignon, he was shocked to see the "miserable honeymooners" approaching their table!

Ramone continued around the table, and Nicole leaned over and whispered to Tim, "I believe God is answering our prayers! Maybe we can form a friendship during the meal." The couples spent the meal getting to know one another. One couple, the Andersons from Georgia, had been on a cruise once every year for ten years and gave them all kinds of useful advice. Another couple, the Brinkleys from South Carolina, had been saving for years to be able to celebrate their twentieth anniversary on this cruise. The last couple, the miserable honeymooners, just sat quietly eating, while the others talked and laughed all through the meal. Finally, Tim asked the husband where they were from and for their names.

He growled in response, "I'm Mark Craddock, and this is my wife, Mitsi. We're from New York and prefer to be left alone."

"Well, I think that since all of us will be dining at the same table all week, the least we can do is get along. May I ask what you two do for a living?" Tim inquired.

"Investments, and Mitsi is going to be staying at home as a domestic engineer."

"Wow, can't say that I know much about the field of investments. By the way, what's everyone doing for their excursion in Cozumel tomorrow? Nicole and I are going to that eco park where they have a natural lazy river, dolphins, and wildlife. I think it's called XCaret," Tim said to get the attention off the

Craddocks. It turned out that the Andersons had not signed up for an excursion; they were planning on just walking around, looking in the shops near the port, and later returning to the ship to hang out. The Brinkleys had signed up to rent four-wheelers and to do a self-guided tour of the island. Tim and Nicole had to chuckle when they found out that the Craddocks had signed up for XCaret too.

When the delectable dinner was finished, Tim and Nicole excused themselves and walked out onto the deck to watch the ocean at night. They were surprised to discover that the ship was pulling into the port at Cozumel. Nicole looked at Tim and rolled her eyes as she said, "Can you believe that we're assigned to the same table as the Crabby Craddocks and signed up to go on the same excursion tomorrow? I'd say God's shouting at us to talk to them. It's sad to think that there must be many other couples onboard who are just as miserable as they seem to be."

"Crabby Craddocks? I love it!" Tim chuckled as he drew Nicole into his arms. "You'd better be careful not to call them that tomorrow. I'd hate to think what Mark would do. We'll look for them on purpose, and hopefully we'll get a chance to witness to them at the park. Now let's forget about them and spend some quality time as husband and wife."

They were awakened the next morning by yet another announcement from Big A1 about the day's activities. At nine thirty, they once again found themselves in another line to disembark for the XCaret excursion. To disembark, they had to scan their key cards and put their sling backpacks on a conveyor belt for the security officer to screen. Once they made it through security, they stepped onto the gangplank and had their picture taken by the ship's photographer. Tim commented to Nicole, "Now I know how an ant feels."

"What on earth...what do you mean by that?"

"Well, just like an ant is minuscule in size compared to me or you, that's what we are compared to the size of this ship. Look at the time, security took longer than I expected. We're gonna have to walk fast to make it to our tour group on time."

They were out of breath when they arrived at the end of the long concrete pier. People were milling around everywhere looking for their tour groups and shopping in the open-air stores that are always present along any port. They heard a Mexican man shouting, "XCaret party over here!" They turned and saw him holding a sign announcing their tour. They approached, gave their names, and were given stickers that simply read, "XCaret." The man pointed them to a group of benches where others were also waiting. Not seeing the Craddocks in the mob of people, they found a bench that was in the shade since the sun was bright and the air humid. They could see the ship from where they were sitting and enjoyed watching the people streaming off. Again, they were reminded of ants that form a line to carry a morsel of food to the ant mound. The people disembarking were in lines and, in comparison to the ship, looked like specks. They also enjoyed listening to all of the sounds and seeing all of the different ethnicities represented around them.

Finally, after a twenty-minute wait, a small blue boat arrived at the pier. The Beauforts were surprised to find that they were taking a ferry over to the mainland of Mexico and to XCaret. They spotted the Craddocks sitting near the back corner of the full, all-enclosed ferry, so Nicole and Tim made their way to them. There weren't many seats left, but Nicole was pleasantly surprised when Mark stood and said, "Here, Mrs. Beaufort, you can sit by Mitsi. I wanted to stand at the front anyway, but Mitsi was too afraid."

"Thanks, Mark. Hey, Mitsi, can't say as I blame you for sitting back here. I'd rather sit here in the back too. Boy, am I glad they have air-conditioning in here! I was starting to get hot while we were waiting for this ferry. So, are you having a nice time on the cruise?"

Mitsi shrugged and replied, "I suppose."

"Tim and I seem to bump into you two everywhere we go. Must say Mark always seems upset 'bout something. Is he always that way?"

This time, Mitsi breathed a long sigh and shrugged while answering, "Yeah, I guess so. He wasn't always like this. He was so sweet when we were dating, but once we got to the ship, he changed. Oh no."

"What's wrong?"

"I hope we're almost there. I'm getting really sick to my stomach. I have a touch of motion sickness.

The cruise ship hasn't bothered me, but this bouncing is making my stomach roll."

"You gonna make it? I think I saw a restroom when we boarded."

"My stomach is just rolling. I don't think I'm going to need a restroom. Let's talk about something else to get my mind off of it."

Remembering she had been looking for an opportunity to talk one on one with Mitsi and remembering how her father would always seize any opportunity to witness, Nicole decided to follow his godly example, took a deep breath and jumped right in to witnessing to her. "Okay...Mitsi, I know we haven't known each other long, but may I ask you a personal question?"

"I guess so."

"If you were to die today, can you show me from the Bible that you know for sure that you'd go to heaven?"

"I sure hope I am."

"Would you like for me to show you how you can know one hundred percent for sure?" At Mitsi's nod, Nicole pulled out her small New Testament from her fanny pack and had the joy of leading Mitsi to Jesus right there on the ferry! Mitsi had just finished asking Jesus to take away her sins and save her when the captain announced that they had arrived. Nicole, with tears in her eyes, gave Mitsi a huge hug and said, "We're sisters now, and the angels in heaven are rejoicing because you accepted Jesus!"

Mitsi was wiping her own tears from her eyes

when Mark approached, reached for her hand, and snarled, "Let's go. I want to be the first ones off this boat." As they rushed off, Mitsi turned and winked at Nicole. Nicole was amazed at the change that had already taken place on Mitsi's face.

"What's the big grin for, Nicky? Miss me already?" Tim joked as he made his way back to Nicole.

"Well, I did miss you, but you're not gonna believe what just happened!" Nicole launched into rapid-fire speech as she shared with Tim the miracle that she had just been allowed to be a part of.

"Oh, Nicky, that's marvelous! God answered our prayers! I wish I could say the same thing happened with Mark. It was like talking to a rock. He just ignored me whenever I'd try to start a conversation with him. We'll keep praying for him. Oh, I'm so proud of you!" Tim exclaimed as he threw his arm around Nicole's shoulder and gave her a quick kiss on the nose.

Chapter 5

When Nicole and Tim entered XCaret, they discovered that it was full of exotic animals, and they were amazed at the variety of colors of the flowers and animals. The park had the look and feel of a Mayan village, and the Beauforts tried to do as much as they could in the small amount of time they had before the bus would leave to take them back to the ferry. They decided to begin with the natural underground lazy river. It took them longer to reach it than they had thought because they kept getting distracted by the beauty of the different animals.

Once at the entrance of the river, they found that they were required to wear life jackets for the swim. They then had to decide which river they wanted to swim—the first was underground the whole time, while the second was partly underground and partly out in the open. They chose to go with the second river so they could enjoy the sun. They put on their life jackets and jumped into the refreshing cool water. They were amazed at how long the swim lasted. It took them over an hour to finish the course. The river led them through canyons and caves, and occasionally it would take them under a light waterfall. At the end of the swim, they were delighted to discover that the river had taken them to a lagoon area at the edge of the ocean where many people were enjoying the day in the sun.

"What did ya think, hon?" Tim asked as he removed his life jacket.

"That was awesome but tiring! I'm exhausted, even though I had to hardly move due to the current pushing me right along. What time do we swim with the dolphins?"

"We have a little over an hour before our scheduled time. Why do you ask?"

"Well, I'm famished after that swim. Is there anywhere to eat in here?"

"I'm sure we can find something. I'm a little hungry myself. Let's see what we can find," Tim replied as he pulled out his park map.

"Well, I need to find a restroom too so I can fix my makeup. I must look a sight."

"Nicky, you're just gonna get wet again when we swim with the dolphins later. Everyone here is walking around wet. Don't worry 'bout it. Besides, you look beautiful to me."

"Oh, all right, if you say so. Did you find us a restaurant yet?"

"Yep, let's go."

Tim led them to an open-air restaurant that overlooked the lagoon. The roof was made of thatch, and live parrots were perched along the perimeter of the restaurant watching the people eat. A bird would occasionally swoop in and land on their table looking for a handout.

When the first bird landed, Nicole shuddered and said, "Can't say that I've ever eaten anywhere quite like this before. The view is just like a picture postcard, but I'm not sure how sanitary it is having birds land on our table."

"Just remember what the Andersons told us at dinner last night—don't order water or ice. We don't want to spend the rest of our cruise with stomach cramps."

They ordered their lunch and were delighted with the authentic Mexican meal. Because of the laid-back nature of the restaurant staff, they were shocked to discover that an entire hour had already passed when they paid the check. They quickly rushed to the section of the park where the dolphin swim was located.

Swimming with the dolphins was their favorite part of the entire day. Listening to the dolphins clicking and chattering and getting to feed them was unlike anything either of them had ever done. By the time the swim was over, it was time to head back to the bus that would take them to the ferry.

They were one of the first couples on the ferry and tried to save the Craddocks a seat. "Tim, can you believe we never once saw Mitsi or Mark? Wonder what they did all day?"

"Whatever they did, I'm sure Mark made it a miserable day for Mitsi. Oh, there they are getting on now!"

Nicole stood up and waved until Mitsi spotted her. Nicole watched as Mitsi and Mark headed over to them.

"Oh, Nicole, thanks for saving us seats. We thought they'd all be taken since we almost didn't make it on time. How was your day?"

They spent the ride back to Cozumel sharing stories from the excursion. The Craddocks had just walked around the park, and they had chosen to swim in the river that was underground the whole time. After hearing Tim and Nicole go on and on about swimming with the dolphins, the Craddocks wished they would have signed up for that too. The closer they got back to Cozumel, though, the paler Mitsi became.

"Mitsi, you're looking awfully pale. Are you okay? Is your stomach still bothering you?" Nicole inquired.

"Oh, yes. It never did settle down from this morning, and now this trip is making it twice as bad. I feel awful."

"Tim, didn't you pick up a motion sickness patch from the ship's pharmacy? We've been fine, so why don't you give it to Mitsi? She really needs it."

"Man, I'd forgotten all about that! It's here in my fanny pack somewhere. I wanted to have one just in case the ferry made us sick. Here it is, you're welcome to use it. The pharmacist said it takes about an hour or so to really kick in," Tim said as he handed the patch to Mitsi.

After looking at Mark for approval, Mitsi eagerly

took it and applied it to the skin behind her ear. "Oh, thank you! I hope it helps. I don't want to be sick all week!"

The ferry finally made it back to Cozumel, so they walked down the long pier back to the ship where they once again had to go through a security checkpoint. They stayed together until they reached their cabins. There they made plans to walk down to dinner together.

Nicole and Tim went to their cabin and discovered that Alfonso, the steward, had left them an octopus made out of bath towels on their bed. "I wish I knew how they made these animals. I'm going to have to go to one of the classes on making towel animals that Big A1 has scheduled. Oh no! I don't think we have enough time to get ready for dinner! We'd better hurry, Tim!" They showered, changed for the formal dinner, and went back to the Craddock's cabin door. At their knock, a frazzled-looking Mark opened the door.

"Sorry, guys. Go on without us. Mitsi is feeling worse. We're going to order room service."

"Oh, I hate to hear that! Do you want me to stay with her?" Nicole offered.

"Nah, we'll be fine. Just go on."

Nicole and Tim tried to enjoy the festivities that accompanied dinner, but they kept worrying about Mitsi. While they were eating their chocolate melting cake for dessert, Mark came rushing up to the table and blurted out, "Nicole, Tim, I don't know what to do. I can't get Mitsi to wake up!"

Overhearing Mark, Ramone picked up a wall phone. When he hung up, he said, "Sir, the doctor will meet you at your cabin. He'll know what to do for your wife."

"Wait, Mark! We're going with you!" Nicole said. They rushed to the elevators, but they were stopped at the very top, so they ran up the stairs to their deck and to the Craddock's cabin. When they arrived, they discovered a white-haired gentleman sitting on the bed next to Mitsi.

"Allow me to introduce myself. I'm Dr. Joseph Lehue. Which one of you is Mr. Craddock?"

"I am, Doctor. How is she? What's wrong with her?" Mark demanded.

"I'm afraid I have some really bad news. Please take a seat." Once Mark was seated, the doctor continued, "I'm afraid your wife has died. I am so sorry for your loss. I understand you were newlyweds."

"Dead? Did you say dead? How could that be?" Mark shouted as he jumped to his feet. "What did you give to her? She only had an upset stomach, and now she's dead? No, something's seriously wrong here!"

Chapter 6

"Doctor Lehue, we were with Mitsi today, and all she ever complained about was an upset stomach from motion sickness. Do you have any idea what could've caused this to happen?" Tim inquired.

The doctor sighed, scratched his head, and replied, "I wish I knew, but right now it appears to be a normal death."

"Normal? She's twenty-seven years old! How does a twenty-seven-year-old die of a natural death?" Mark demanded.

"I agree, sir, and I assure you that I will be performing an autopsy. A ship security officer, Mr. Rick Ortega, will be here shortly. He'll need to check into a few things. It's normal procedure whenever we have a death onboard. Now, I need to ask all of you to step outside while my assistant and I take care of Mrs. Craddock."

Nicole and Tim tried talking Mark into going with them to their cabin, but he told them that he'd rather be by himself and that he was going to the grand lobby. As they watched him walk away, Nicole told Tim, "How awful! To only be married for three days! At least, he has a peaceful last image of her. She looked like she had just fallen asleep."

"Yeah, I know what you mean. I'm curious to see what the autopsy turns up," Tim said as he led Nicole out onto the balcony.

Nicole sat down and asked, "Why? What are you thinking?"

"Well, maybe I'm just paranoid after all that happened in Pilotview this last year, but their relationship has been strange since we first met them, and now she dies unexpectedly? It sounds awfully suspicious to me!"

"Oh, Tim, I hope not! I really don't want to go through another investigation. And we don't even have Shelly and Curly here to help us! Oh! You know what I just thought of? I just remembered that Mitsi is in heaven right now because she accepted Jesus as her Savior today. She's at peace and happy right now! Boy, am I glad I got up the nerve to witness to her. I don't think I could've lived with myself if she had died, and I had never told her about the Lord."

"Yeah, now you know you'll see her again. Not to change the subject, hon, but—" Tim was interrupted by a knock at the door. He went and looked through the peephole to see an officer on the other side. He opened the door and asked, "Yes, may I help you?"

"Hello, I'm Mr. Ortega, the head security officer. I understand you were with Mr. and Mrs. Craddock today. May I come in and ask you a few questions?"

"Sure, come on in. Let me get my wife from the balcony."

After Tim and Nicole were seated on the couch, Mr. Ortega began, "I understand that Mitsi wasn't feeling well today?"

Nicole answered, "That's right. The ferry's bouncing gave her motion sickness. She wasn't too bad on the way over, but on the way back, she got really sick."

"Did she take anything for it?"

Tim spoke up. "Yes, sir. I had a motion sickness patch with me. When I gave it to her, she put it on right away, but it didn't seem to ever help."

"Was this patch one you brought from home?"

"No, sir. When I heard we had to take a ferry to go to XCaret, I went to the pharmacy and asked for one. I wasn't sure if either one of us would do well on a smaller boat."

"Okay. Now how about Mr. and Mrs. Craddock's relationship? How would you describe it?"

Nicole sighed and answered, "Oh, well, I hate to speak badly of others, but it wasn't that good."

"What do you mean by 'wasn't that good'? How bad was it?"

"Well, I first met them in line at Port Canaveral, and when I started talking to Mitsi, Mark told her to leave us alone. Then later we saw them arguing in the hallway outside their cabin. Every time we saw them, they were either arguing or not speaking to each other. They didn't act like newlyweds should."

"Is there anything else you can think of that I might need to know?" When Nicole and Tim both shook their heads no, he continued, "If you think of anything, and I mean anything, please don't hesitate to contact me. You can ask your steward to get a message to me. Thank you for your time."

After he left, Tim reminded Nicole, "Didn't you want to call home tonight? It's getting late, so you'd better call now if you're going to."

"Oh my! I'd completely forgotten with all that's happened. She'll probably think I've forgotten her. Where did I put my cell? Boy, am I glad I got a phone that was global when I did my last upgrade! And the funny part was I had no idea! Oh, duh, I forgot I put it in the room safe so no one would see it. I just hope Dad is still having good days and doing okay." Nicole went to the safe, entered her code, removed her phone, and called home. "Shell, is that you? Can you hear me okay?"

"Nicole! I hear you fine. You called at just the right time. I was just getting ready for bed. Max, hush! I can't hear Nicole! Sorry, Nicole, Max is trying to get my bedtime snack. I want to hear all about your trip. How's it going?"

"Oh, the trip has been beautiful! But you're not going to believe what's happened..." Nicole went on to tell Shelly all about the ship and the excursion. She then told her about the Craddocks and about how she had led Mitsi to the Lord earlier in the day. She ended by telling Shelly about the terrible ending to the day and how the security officer had just left.

"She died? Oh, Nicole, how awful for her husband! How's he taking it?" Shelly asked.

"Hard to say. He's down in the lobby right now.

He's a strange person. Listen, this is going to cost me a fortune, but before I get off, I need to know how Dad's doing. Is everything going okay? Any problems?"

Shelly assured Nicole that she and Tucker were handling Mr. Sheldon just fine and were, in fact, having fun with him and that her dad was, in fact, having quite an enjoyable time playing fetch with Max.

"Shell, speaking of Tucker, isn't tomorrow your court date? What are you going to do with Dad?"

"Oh, the pastor asked one of the men from church to come and sit with him."

"That's good. So are you excited about tomorrow?"

Shelly sighed. "Oh, Nicole, I'm trying to not get my hopes up. You know how this adoption process has been going on ever since his granddad gave me permission to adopt him, but the courts are taking forever to process things. They've already continued it twice. Listen to me go on! I forgot that you're calling from a ship in the middle of the Caribbean! Listen, everything is fine here. Don't worry about a thing and don't bother calling unless there's a problem, okay? I'll be praying for Mr. Craddock and y'all. Bye now. Give Tim my love."

"Will do, Shell. Bye." Nicole felt much better after talking with her best friend. After she hung up, Tim reminded her that they were going on another excursion the next day and needed to get their rest.

Chapter 7

The next day, they had arrived at Belize and had signed up for a tour of the Mayan ruins. The ferry that took them from the ship to the shore was a different experience than the one in Cozumel. This one was a large motorboat and was very noisy. When they stepped off the ferry, Nicole had to laugh at how soaked Tim had gotten from the spray from the boat; he looked like he had showered in his clothes.

The group touring the ruins had to first travel upriver, so when a smaller motorboat pulled up at the dock, the group was directed to get onboard. Nicole could not help but think of Mitsi and how sick the boat would have made her if she had been there. As the boat first headed off, Nicole kept trying to keep her hair in some semblance of order, but she soon realized that it was going to be a losing battle. At the speed they were going, the wind was whipping her hair all over the place. Tim just laughed, pulled her into a hug, and told her to quit worrying so much.

The ride up the River Wallace was very relaxing and enjoyable. The guide had the driver slow down at the point where the ocean and the river meet so they could look for manatees. Tim kept grabbing Nicole's arm and pointing at the ocean, but by the time she looked, the manatee would be back underwater. Nicole never did see one; Tim assured her that she had not missed much because they resembled logs in the water. As the boat picked up speed and headed upriver, everyone onboard was looking for crocodiles. The driver and guide assured them that they always spotted them, but no crocodiles were out on their ride. At one point, they went under a bridge, and Nicole let out a loud shriek when she looked up and saw that the underside was covered with bats.

The boat arrived at a restaurant, which seemed to them to be in the middle of the jungle. As they were walking up steps dug out of the side of the riverbank, they heard noises coming from the trees overhead. When they looked up, they were delighted to discover monkeys playing.

"Oh, Tim, this is so awesome! I wish I could bring my second graders here to see this! Wouldn't that be a great field trip? Oh, look! There's a baby monkey sleeping next to its mama!"

"I agree. This is a wonderful place. I'm just hoping that the restaurant has air-conditioning. I'd have to say that Belize definitely has North Carolina beat for humidity. I'm completely dry after being so wet earlier. Come on, let's go get something to eat. Maybe we'll be able to see the monkeys from inside."

They entered a thatch-covered hut that had a screened porch running its length. Once inside, Tim had to chuckle when he realized that there was no air-conditioning, but there were plenty of open windows and ceiling fans running on high, so the meal ended up being quite pleasant.

Remembering to stick with bottled sodas, they ordered a hamburger and fries, and after they ate, they went outside to explore the grounds. They discovered several booths set up at the front entrance with handmade local crafts. By the time Nicole had purchased souvenirs for all of her friends and family, it was time to load the bus for the ride to the ruins.

They were riding to the ruins with another group that had met up with them at the restaurant, and Tim and Nicole were thrilled to find the Andersons already onboard. Candy Anderson motioned for them to sit beside them near the back of the bus.

"How y'all doin'? Can ya believe this heat? I thought Georgia was bad, but this is just like bein' in a sauna. This here air-conditioned bus still feels hot to me." Candy started chattering as Nicole and Tim were getting situated in their seats. She continued without a breath, "Isn't it just plumb awful about Mitsi? I's a just tellin' Victor here that I wouldn't be surprised at all if that mean ole husband of hers murdered her. Isn't he just the most hatefulest man you ever did see? And to be honeymooners at that! Huh! They act like theys been married fer fifty years or more. Ouch! I wish our driver would keep his eyes open and avoid these potholes. I declare, I's never been on such a bumpy bus ride before."

Nicole chuckled and replied, "I'm trying not to watch after I saw him almost blindside a car a little way back. I have to agree with you about it being a shame that Mitsi's gone. I hope you're wrong about her husband, though."

"Well, maybe I am. Could be, especially after what I heard 'bout Barry Schmidt. Have y'all heard yet?"

"Barry? What about him?" Tim asked.

"Oh my! Y'all hadn't heard? Well, our steward told me this mornin' that the poor doctor is just overwhelmed and worn out because of Mitsi dying yesterday and now Barry. Seems he was found in the spa sprawled out on a massage table dead."

"What? Barry's dead too? What on earth! Do they have any idea what happened? Maybe he had a heart attack," Tim suggested.

"Well, I couldn't get the steward to say, but it just seems mighty suspicious to me that two people have died in just two days. We're planning on being real careful like, don't we, Victor?"

"Yes, dear," Victor replied without even opening his eyes as he napped.

"Wow! I sure wasn't expecting to hear that. I wonder how his wife Janet is doing," Nicole asked.

"Don't know. How'd ya know his wife's name?"

Tim responded, "Oh, we know them from back home. They have two young boys."

"Oh, them poor things! To lose your pa like this! And you knew them? If I's you, I'd be real careful. You've known both of the people murdered. For all you know, you could be next on his list."

Nicole shuddered, snuggled closer to Tim, and whispered, "I don't like this at all. I really wish Curly and Shelly were here to help us."

"Me too, hon, me too," Tim replied.

Chapter 8

Candy's announcement had a dampening effect on Nicole and Tim's afternoon at the Mayan ruins. They halfheartedly listened to their guide in the sweltering humidity as he droned on and on about the Mayan culture and what the different remaining ruins had been used for during that time period. When the guide finally came to a stop and offered to let the tourists climb the steps to the top of the tallest ruin on that site, Tim turned to Nicole and asked, "What do you think? Want to go up there and see what it looks like, hon?"

"If you are wanting to, I'll be glad to go. But don't feel like you need to because of me. It doesn't matter to me one way or another. I've never really been much of a history buff. Honestly, the whole time the guide was talking, I kept thinking of two little boys who've just lost their daddy. I wish we could just go back to the ship."

"I'm with you. It won't bother me to miss walking up all those steps. Why don't we just head back to the bus and wait for everyone there?" He held out his hand, and when she grabbed it, they leisurely walked toward the bus. Once there, they realized that the closed-up bus was too stuffy after it had been sitting in the hot Belize sun, so they found a tree nearby to sit under.

"You know, something Candy said has stuck with me."

"What would that be?" Nicole asked as she poured some water out of her water bottle onto her neck.

"Remember when she said that we know both victims? I have a feeling that we're going to be seeing Officer Ortega again. I'm beginning to wish we had gone to Gatlinburg instead of coming on this cruise. This honeymoon is turning into a nightmare. The company is the best anyone could ask for, but the unfolding drama is starting to creep me out. I'm so sorry this is happening, honey."

"Like it's your fault? Don't you worry 'bout me. I'm pretty tough. I just pray they find out what's going on soon. Maybe we're just overreacting, and both deaths are natural ones."

"Yeah, maybe, but it would be a strange coincidence, wouldn't it? Two people we know dying within a day of each other? Oh, look! There's our group headed this way. Let's get on the bus and get a seat all to ourselves. I don't feel up to hearing anymore of Mrs. Anderson's chatter."

They boarded the bus, settled into their seats, and quickly fell asleep in the stifling heat for a much-needed nap. When they awoke, they discovered that the bus had returned them to their ferry. Once back on ship, they headed straight for their cabin. As they approached their cabin, Nicole spotted a piece of paper stuck to the door.

"Wonder what this is about?" Nicole mused out loud as she pulled it off. She started opening it as they entered their cabin. Once Tim pulled the door shut, she read out loud, "Mr. and Mrs. Beaufort, please dial extension nine-two-seven upon your return. I have some questions that I need to ask you. Sincerely, Mr. Ortega."

"Oh, great! Now for more questioning! Hopefully he'll let us eat our dinner first because I would like to relax in some air-conditioning and get something cold to drink after all of that heat today," Tim replied as he picked up the phone to call the security officer. He punched the number into the phone sitting on the desk and asked for Mr. Ortega.

He arranged for the interview to take place in their cabin after their evening meal. "Okay, Nicky, that's taken care of. Let's freshen up and head to dinner."

They were the last to arrive at their table and were delighted to discover that the waiter had already poured their sodas for them. As he pulled the chair out for Nicole, Tim leaned next to her ear and whispered, "Everyone seems sort of subdued, don't they?"

"Oh, there y'all are! I was just finishin' tellin' the rest of our little group 'bout what happened to that poor Mr. Schmidt!" Candy said as Tim sat down.

Before he could reply, Becky Main shuddered and said, "Oh, that poor man's family! Roger, dear, we need to go by their room later and offer her our help. What do you think?" She turned and looked to him for confirmation.

"Yes, dear, I agree. As soon as we've finished eating, we'll find our steward and ask him for their cabin number. I mean her cabin number," Roger answered as he put more salt onto his potato before continuing to eat.

"Rats, I wish we could go with y'all." Nicole interrupted. "But we need to talk to Mr. Ortega after we eat."

"Mr. Ortega? Ain't he that interfering security officer?" Mark Craddock spit out. "He keeps hounding me, telling me he thinks that I had somethin' to do with Mitsi's death! I just got married! Why would I kill her?"

"I just thought of something, Mark!" Tim exclaimed. "Now that Barry has, um, died, Officer Ortega surely can't be suspecting you. That is, unless you knew the Schmidts." Tim watched him shake his head before continuing. "It seems obvious to me that he'll at least be suspicious that these two deaths are related. And if you didn't know them, then you don't have a motive for killing them. Thus, you are off the hook!"

"Well, I certainly hope he thinks like you do," Mark growled as he stood to his feet, threw his napkin onto his plate, and continued, "I'm out of here. I'm going to hit the casinos for a few hours."

"My, my, he sure isn't acting like any grieving widowers that I've known," Roger Main said.

"Now, dear, you know that everyone responds to tragedy differently. Remember how your cousin Fred went wild after his sweet wife passed on? And then, after a year, it finally hit him that she was really gone, and he fell apart?" Becky admonished as she patted her husband's hand.

"Just saying that I don't believe I'd go to a casino the day after you died when I'd only been married a day. You know?" Roger asked while looking around at the rest of the couples while shrugging his shoulders.

"I'm with you, Roger." Tim spoke up as he pushed his chair back to stand. "I'm a newlywed of just three days, and I know for a fact that I'd be hiding away in my cabin if something had happened to Nicky only one day into our marriage." He looked at his watch and turned to Nicole. "Nicky, we need to hurry if we're gonna be on time for our meeting with Mr. Ortega." He helped her out of her seat and offered her his arm before turning to leave.

They exited the dining room, and once on the elevator, she leaned her head against his shoulder and sighed. "Hon, while you were telling Mark Craddock that he has nothing to worry about, I kept hearing Mrs. Anderson telling us that you knew both of the victims! What if Mr. Ortega suspects you? I don't want anything to happen to you! I'm starting to agree that we should've gone to Gatlinburg."

Tim put his arm around her, pulled her close, and replied, "Me? What motive could he think that I would have? I think you're just overreacting. You'll see." As the elevator doors opened, he dropped a quick kiss onto her forehead and continued, "I'm sure he is just wanting information from me since I'm a social worker. Come on, he's probably waiting for us." Tim took her hand and led her to their cabin. As he was unlocking the door, they could hear Nicole's cell phone ringing.

"That's Shelly's ring! With all that's been going on, I totally forgot that she was calling after her court date," Nicole yelled out as she rushed to the safe but was unable to get the phone out before it stopped ringing. "What should I do? Should I call her back right now or wait until after our meeting?"

Before he could respond, they heard a knock at the door. "Guess that's your answer. Since that's probably him, just wait until afterward. That way you'll be able to tell her everything and not have to rush," Tim answered as he opened the door and invited Mr. Ortega into the cabin. "May I get you a Coke or some water, sir?"

"No, thank you. I would like to get right into things. Please be seated, Mr. and Mrs. Beaufort. I've brought a recorder with me and will be recording this interview." After switching the tiny device on and stating the date and time, he continued, "Mr. Beaufort, I need to inform you that a Mr. Barry Schmidt died of an apparent heart attack today. Mitsi Craddock died yesterday after returning from an excursion to XCaret. I have been informed that she was poisoned, and the poison was administered through the motion sickness patch that you gave to her. I have just learned that Mr. Schmidt also died from this same poison. I am heading this investigation until we return to port in Florida, at which point this investigation will be turned over to the FBI. I am hoping that by that time, I will be able to hand them the suspect. I have already spoken with your dining companions, and they informed me that Mr. Schmidt had told them how he and his wife knew you. As I understand it, Mr. Schmidt rather hated you for removing his children from his home and the part you played in the Department of Social Services investigation into his family. Due to these factors, I am officially informing you that you are a person of interest in this investigation since you had means and opportunity for both deaths and a motive for the one. If you choose to not answer my questions completely and honestly, which is your right, I will immediately detain you for the duration of this cruise until the FBI can do their own investigation."

"What?" Nicole and Tim both shouted together. Nicole reached over, grabbed Tim's hand, and squeezed hard.

"Go ahead, Mr. Ortega. I have nothing to hide. It's okay, Nicky," Tim replied after seeing the stark terror on her face. "I want answers the same as you do."

Chapter 9

Hearing Nicole's voicemail message start, Shelly clicked off her cell and turned to Tucker. "I've got a great idea! Let's go surprise Curly at his office and tell him our great news!"

"Sure, Miss Gale, but I thought you already called and told him all 'bout it," Tucker replied as he tossed Max his favorite squeaky toy while his orange kitten, Garfield, chased after the laser light he was flashing on the floor.

"Oh, I did try earlier, but he was out on a call, and this is something that I want to share in person. I'm about ready to burst from excitement and haven't been able to get a hold of anyone to share it with! Come on, let's get going!" Shelly picked up her pocketbook, cell phone, car keys, and locked the door behind Tucker.

Once in the car, she looked over at him and asked, "So we both know how excited I am, but how about you? How are you feeling about all of this?"

Tucker giggled and replied, "You're excited? Wow! I woulda never have known!" He laughed as Shelly punched him on the shoulder. "Seriously? I'm ways past excited, but with all that's gone wrong in my life, I was just expectin' more bad news today. Actually, I'm almost 'fraid to get too excited in case something else happens to mess it all up."

Shelly reached over, squeezed his shoulder, and responded, "Now I know it's been a really, really rough year for you, but that's starting to sound like superstition. As a Christian, we know that God is in control of this situation and that nothing can happen to you without Him allowing it. Oh, we're here. Come on, I can't wait to see the look on Curly's face when we tell him."

As they entered the front entrance to the police station, the officer at the front desk called out, "Hey, Miss Gale and Tucker! Good to see y'all! Curly just got back. You'll find him in his office. You can go on back." The officer reached over and pushed a button to open the door to the back offices.

"I'm glad it's a quiet evening in here," Shelly whispered, leaning over to Tucker as they made their way down the hall.

"This place gives me the creeps no matter how many times I've been here with y'all," Tucker whispered back as Shelly knocked on Curly's door.

"Come on in, it's open!" Curly shouted from inside. When he looked up and saw it was Shelly and Tucker, he jumped up and said, "Hey, y'all! I saw your number on my caller ID, Shell, and was just gettin' ready to call you back. You didn't leave a message. What's up?"

"Oh, Curly! I've been dying to tell somebody!" Shelly answered as she excitedly twisted her pocketbook in her hands.

"Well, judgin' from the grins on yer faces, I'm assumin' you had a good day in court?"

"Not just a good day, we had a great day! The judge finally terminated Mitch's parental rights. Not only that, but after hearing that both sets of grandparents are in agreement with me adopting Tucker, he approved the motion to adopt! Can you believe it? After all this time and postponed court dates? All that's left is for the paperwork to come from Raleigh! I am officially Tucker's mother as of today!"

Curly pulled her into a big hug and said, "Oh, wow! That's great, Shell! God really answered our prayers!" Pulling back, he reached over for Tucker and asked, "What about you? Are you as excited as Miss Gale? Or should I say your mom?" He laughed as Shelly squealed and asked again, "Well?"

"Yes, sir. I'm excited too. I'mma just afraid that somethin' bad's gonna happen to mess things up. But Miss Gale keeps tellin' me that God's in control, and I'm tryin' hard to trust Him."

"You don't have anything to worry about. It's pretty much a done deal now that the judge has approved the motion. So, Shell, what did Nicole say when you told her about it? I'm surprised I didn't hear her screaming all the way from her ship," Curly asked with a chuckle.

"Well, I tried to call her earlier too, but she must still be at dinner 'cause all I got was her voicemail. That's why we came here. I was dying to share the news with someone, and all I was getting were voicemails. Maybe she'll see I called and call me back soon."

"I must say that I am thrilled she didn't answer. It always brightens my day to see you and Tucker. What do you say to heading over to the ice cream shop to celebrate? My treat!"

"All right! Can I get a banana split?" Tucker asked as they headed for Shelly's ever dependable rusty Accord.

"Sure, son, sure." After they were in the car and buckled up, Curly looked over at Shelly and asked, "Um, Shell, do you have any plans for this weekend?"

"No, why?"

"I want to take you out somewhere really nice to celebrate your being a mom. What do you think about going to Ryan's on Saturday night?"

"Mmm, that place is wonderful! I'd love to, but you don't have to go that extravagant!"

"It's my pleasure. I'm sure that Tucker would rather not go with us on a mushy date, so I'll check with my brother, Craig, and see if Tucker can go over to his house to play some head-to-head on Xbox. He's always telling me how much he likes Tucker, so I'm sure it won't be a problem."

"Thanks for not making me go along on a date with y'all. I'm still trying to get over going along with her and Mr. Beaufort on that date to the mall! Man, that was so embarrassing!" Tucker said from the backseat.

Laughing, Curly reached over for Shelly's hand, winked, and replied, "I'm really glad that date didn't work out. Trust me, one day you'll enjoy going out with a beautiful lady, but I understand where you're coming from. We're here. Look at this place! It's crowded as usual! Oh, well, their ice cream is worth the wait." Curly walked around and opened Shelly's door for her and had to laugh as Tucker went running off when he spotted one of his school buddies.

Just as they took their place in line, Shelly heard her cell phone ringing. Pulling it out of her pocketbook, she saw that it was Nicole and turned to Curly. "Just order me a single scoop of peanut butter cup. It's Nicole."

Walking over to the car to get some privacy, Shelly answered the phone, "Hello? Nicole? Guess what? I'm a mom!"

Shelly laughed as Nicole squealed before answering, "Oh, Shell! I'm so thrilled for you! It finally happens, and it has to be when I'm half a world away! I hate to bring you down on such a wonderful day, but you're never going to believe what just happened! The cruise ship's security officer just told Tim that he is the number one suspect in two deaths that have taken place onboard! What am I gonna do?"

Chapter 10

After talking with Shelly about all that had been happening on ship, Nicole leaned against Tim, sighed, and said, "I really wish they could be here with us. We could use Curly's help with that security officer, and I miss having Shell's support. Don't take me wrong, you're wonderful—"

Interrupting, Tim calmed her. "It's okay, Nicky, I understand. I'd be jealous if you were saying things were going well, but with Mr. Ortega suspecting me of murder, I understand why you'd want your best friend here." Tim twirled a strand of her blond hair between his fingers and groaned out loud, "I can't believe this is happening to us on our honeymoon! Hold on! Wait a minute! I just thought of something! You'd like to have Shelly here, and I could really use Curly's help, right?"

She turned and looked at him confusedly before responding, "Didn't I just say that? But we are out in the middle of the Caribbean, hon."

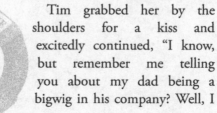

Tim grabbed her by the shoulders for a kiss and excitedly continued, "I know, but remember me telling you about my dad being a bigwig in his company? Well, I just remembered that this cruise line is one of the companies that he owns stock in!"

"Okay... that's great, but what does that have to do with Curly and Shelly being here with us?"

"I'm pretty sure that he owns majority stock, so... maybe, just maybe, he can pull some strings and get the cruise line to allow Curly, Shelly, and Tucker to join us at our next port. I think we're going to Costa Maya next." Tim jumped to his feet and began rummaging through their papers trying to find the itinerary.

"Um, honey? I don't want to shoot such a lovely idea down, but will Tucker be allowed to leave NC when the adoption isn't even final yet? And I just thought of something! Oh, Tim! What if one of us had put that patch on? One of us would be dead! Oh, I hate that anyone died, but to think it could've been one of us! Yes, we definitely need to figure out how to get them here!"

Pulling her into a hug, Tim rubbed his hands up and down her back excitedly. "Oh, wow! I didn't think of that. Makes you realize how precious life is. Let's just take it one step at a time about getting Curly and Shelly here. First step, we really need to take this to the Lord in prayer."

Joining hands, Tim led Nicole in a prayer, asking the Lord for wisdom, guidance, and protection. After ending the prayer, he kissed her on the forehead and said, "Why don't you go on to bed? I'm gonna give Dad a call, and we'll probably be a while. Then, if he thinks he can make this happen, I'm gonna try to call

Curly." He picked up the cell phone and went to the balcony so he wouldn't disturb her while talking.

He found he was holding his breath as he punched in the familiar numbers and waited for someone to pick up on the other end. "Dad? Tim here...well, we've had a couple of problems..."

The next morning, Nicole woke up to an empty bed. Looking around for Tim, she found him out on the balcony with his Bible on his lap. She walked out and gave him a kiss. "Good morning. You're up awfully early. What'd your dad have to say last night?"

"That's why I'm up so early, I can't seem to sleep. He needed some time to check into things on his end. He's supposed to call any minute now to let me know if he can make it happen. Since we're at sea for today, why don't you order us room service for breakfast? That way we won't miss his call."

"Sounds good. Oh, honey, that would be awesome if Curly, Shelly, and Tucker could be here! I didn't even let myself hope for it last night 'cause I thought it was too far-fetched of an idea, but if your father thinks he might be able to make it work..."

Tim smiled while reaching for her hand. "Yeah, he really thinks it's a possibility. Now that sound you hear is my stomach rumblin'. You gonna make me some breakfast, woman?"

Laughing, Nicole smacked him lightly on the shoulder. "Watch it, buster, or you'll never eat! I'm getting pretty hungry myself, so I'll go place the order right now."

While she was on the phone with room service,

she could hear Tim's cell phone ringing. After placing the order, she waited for him to finish before joining him out on the balcony. *Please, Lord, please let this work out. We really need your help and Curly's with this mess we're in. Who would want to kill people while in such a beautiful place?* Seeing him lay his phone on the small table, Nicole went back out to the balcony.

"Breakfast will be here in a few minutes. Was that your father? What'd he say?"

Tim stretched before answering, "He was able to get it all worked out! He's even gonna pay for their plane tickets to Costa Maya! I shared your concern about Tucker leaving North Carolina, and he said that he'd call DSS personally to work things out. Worst- case scenario? Tucker would have to stay a week with his grandfather, which I doubt would be a problem."

"Wow! I can't believe it! Curly and Shelly could be here on this ship tomorrow? Yes!" Shrieking, Nicole jumped up and hugged Tim. "Thank you! You're the best! Remind me to get your father a fantastic thank-you souvenir from one of our stops!"

"Slow down, Nicky. We still have to talk to Curly and Shelly about all of this. They might have other things going on, or Curly might not be able to take time off from the department right now."

"Nah, God's worked this much of it out. I'm sure He's going to work the rest out too. Besides, I know Shell, and she'll be thrilled to help us. Go ahead and call Curly. I'm gonna get ready before room service gets here."

Nicole went and dressed for the day, while Tim placed the call to Curly. Shelly had already updated him on the two deaths, so Tim just had to tell him what his father had planned. After talking through the details, Tim hung up and went to tell Nicole about the call.

Before he could close the balcony door behind him, there was a knock on their room door and someone shouting, "Room service!" Looking at Nicole and shrugging, Tim said, "Let me get that, and then I'll tell you what he had to say." He opened the door for the steward to enter. After the steward had set their breakfast tray down, Tim signed the ticket and locked the door when he left. "Okay, let's talk while we eat. What'd you order me?" Tim pulled the metal lid off and exclaimed, "Yes! Biscuits and gravy! You sure know your husband!"

"Tim! Enough suspense! What did Curly say?"

"What'd you get? Just cereal and fruit? What a wimpy breakfast."

"Tim...I'm warning you..."

"Okay, okay!" Tim threw his hands up. "I surrender to the beautiful lady! He thinks it's a great idea. He's pretty sure that he can rearrange his schedule so he can get a week off. He's planning on calling back as soon as he talks to his captain and Shelly. He said that since Shelly's on summer break, it shouldn't be a problem for her. He's also going to check into Tucker leaving North Carolina and call the pastor to see if someone at the church can watch your dad."

"Who on earth will they find for Dad to stay with? It has to be someone he already knows. I hate being so far from him and not being able to help. Oh, I'm sorry! This is such a mess, and here I am wishing to go home when I'm on my honeymoon! I wish I could cut myself in two and be in two places at once. Tim, I can't stand just sitting here and waiting for the phone to ring. I'm gonna go nutso!"

Laughing while pulling her into a hug, Tim replied, "I feel the same way. Why don't we head up to the Lido Deck? I challenge you to a game of ping-pong. Winner gives the loser a back massage."

"Hmm...ping-pong? I haven't played that in years, but I used to put a mean spin on the ball. It will be a good distraction from the phone too. Okay, you're on! Boy, that back massage is gonna feel heavenly!"

Tim wiped his mouth and rubbed his belly. "That was delicious. Almost as good as my mom's biscuits. I'm ready if you are." He continued after she nodded, "On to the battlefield, my dear!"

Giggling and rolling her eyes, Nicole replied, "Oh, Tim, you are so silly! But that is part of the reason why I love you so much. Just don't forget the room key or the cell phone. I'd hate to miss Curly's call."

They strolled leisurely through the halls and made their way to the Lido Deck. Once at the ping-pong table, they discovered that another young couple was already using it. Seeing that Tim and Nicole were waiting to play, the other couple introduced themselves as Maggy and Luke Tolson and invited them to play doubles with them. They finally decided that the women would be on a team and the men on the other team. After playing a game, they looked around to see that several people had stopped to watch and cheer them on. Tim looked over at Luke and asked, "What do you say we play with a handicap? Beating the women by ten that first game is a little rough, don't you think?"

"What kind of handicap are you talking about?" Luke asked.

"We could play with our opposite hand?"

Hearing someone yell from the crowd, "Don't do it! Play like normal!" Tim turned and saw that Mark Craddock was the one yelling.

"Hey, Mark! It's just a game, and I'd like to be in my wife's good graces afterward!"

Clapping Tim on the back, Luke answered, "I'm with you, man. Let's do it." The men then played the next two games with their opposite hands, but they still managed to beat the women, although the score ended up being a lot closer.

When the third game was over, Nicole laughed and said, "That's enough for me. It was fun, but I hate to lose! It was great meeting y'all. Maybe we can get together again, just not for more ping-pong!"

Maggy replied, "I totally agree! I'm dragging Luke to the class on towel folding after lunch. Want to meet us there?"

"What do you think, Tim?" Nicole asked.

"Sure, why not? I guess it's your turn to torture

us. Besides, every night when you see the new animal housekeeping made out of towels, you say that you wished you knew how to do it. Save us a spot, okay?"

"Will do," Luke answered as he reached out his hand. "See you there."

Watching them walk away, Nicole said, "That was really fun! Guess I owe you a back massage."

"Yep, and be sure I will not let you forget either! Let's go see if we can grab one of those hammocks on Serenity Level. Oh! There's my cell phone! It's Curly!

Chapter 11

Back in Pilotview, Curly and Shelly were frantically packing and making lists of things to do after they gave Tim and Nicole the good news that they were coming to join them at their next stop in Costa Maya. Curly had swapped some of his days with the other detective on the force, and Shelly was able to go since she was on summer break. Mr. Beaufort had scheduled the company jet for them to leave that evening, so they spent the morning dividing up the tasks they had yet to do. Curly volunteered to take Nicole's dad to the family from church that had agreed to care for him.

After looking over their list of things to do again, Shelly said, "Wait a minute, Curly. We forgot about our passports! I already have one from when I went on a mission's trip to Mexico a couple of years ago. What about you?"

"Oh, yeah! I had plumb forgot about passports! Yeah, I have one. About three years ago, I thought about going to Europe for a sightseeing trip, so I went ahead and got it done. Never have used it, though. Better write it down on my list so I don't forget to pick it up at my place. What about Tucker? Does he have one?"

"His grandfather gave it to me back when he moved in with me. Seems like he took the whole family to Europe about a year before Ray and Cheryl died. Okay, good. That's one biggie taken care of. Why don't you go pack and go by your bank after dropping off Mr. Sheldon? After that, meet me back here so Mr. Beaufort can give us a ride to the airport. I believe we are to leave here at five. He said that it's about a six-hour flight. I'll take care of packing the camera and sunscreen."

"All righty, sounds like a plan. See you in a little bit. Can you believe we're gonna be in the Caribbean this time tomorrow, Shell? I just pray we can help them out of this mess they've gotten themselves into." Turning to Mr. Sheldon, Curly raised his voice and continued, "Mr. Sheldon, it's time to go. I've already loaded your suitcase into my car."

"Suitcase? Why do I need my suitcase? Thought you were taking me to see a baseball game," Mr. Sheldon muttered as he struggled to find his shoes.

Shelly picked up his shoes from under the table, handed them to him, and replied, "Mr. Sheldon, I have your shoes. Here. We'll have to go to a baseball game another day. The Cline family from church wants you to come spend a couple of nights with them."

"Cline? Who are they? I don't know any Cline. And where's my Nicky? She promised to take me to Winston-Salem to see the Winston-Salem Dash play baseball today."

"Um...she's on her honeymoon with Tim. Now just go on with Detective Rogers. Have fun," Shelly encouraged. She grinned and shook her head at Curly from behind Mr. Sheldon's back.

Curly opened the door and said firmly, "Come on, Mr. Sheldon. I'm going to take you to visit a wonderful family. You'll love them. They've got two boys..."

Shelly sighed as she watched Curly help him into the car. Lord, it's sad to see a once vibrant man who served you faithfully for so many years start to fade. This Alzheimer's disease is so cruel to rob him of his dignity. If it be possible, could you call him home to you in another way that would be swift and pain free? I sure hate to see him like this, and I know it has to be harder for Nicole. Just watching him for these last few days has been hard for me. I don't know how she does it all the time and remains so happy and upbeat. Well, I do know...you are the answer. You are her strength. Please help us to get them off this security officer's list of suspects. Mr. Sheldon needs his daughter badly. Thank you, Lord, for hearing me and loving me. I sure do love you.

Feeling much better after spending those necessary minutes talking to her Savior, Shelly went to wake Tucker and get them both packed. Tucker woke up quickly and was excited to hear they were going to get to go to the cruise ship. It didn't take them long to pack since Shelly had started to lay out most of their clothing during the early morning. Zipping the last zipper closed, she called for Tucker to carry them out to the front porch.

"Okay, Tucker, I want you to vacuum the

carpeted areas while I straighten up and sweep and mop the kitchen and bathroom. We don't want to leave food crumbs. We'd return to a house of ants."

"Sure, Miss Gale, I mean, huh! I don't know whatta call you now. You're my legal mom and all, but..."

Laughing, Shelly ruffled his hair and interrupted him so she could reassure him. "I'd say stick to Miss Gale, but that will probably be very noticeable onboard the ship and cause comments. Let's see, 'Mama' is always going to be reserved for your first adoptive mother, okay? How about, hmm . . . 'Mama Shelly'?" Shelly asked with a shrug. "Although I'll warn you that it'll take me a while to learn to answer to that name."

"Sure, Mama Shelly works for me. Okay, I'll get to that vacuumin'."

Since her place was so tiny, it didn't take the two of them long to get everything in order. As soon as they had finished, Shelly put their passports in her carry-on bag so they wouldn't be forgotten. Picking up the list she and Curly had written, she turned to Tucker and smiled. "We're getting close! Let's go grab a burger and head on over to my bank. I need to get some traveler's checks. It sure was nice of Tim's dad to give us some spending money. Curly's got some saved up too, so with his money and this from Mr. Beaufort, we should have plenty. Come on, I'm hungry."

Driving to Burger King, Shelly looked at Tucker and noticed that he had a huge smile on his face. "What's that big grin for?"

"What? Oh...it's just so awesome for us to git ta fly in a private jet and git to investigate a murder on a cruise ship! Can't wait ta git back and tell Cody 'bout this! Sure beats his stories about goin' huntin'."

"Us investigate? Now wait just a minute, young man. Curly will be doing all the investigating, understand? This is a very dangerous guy he'll be looking for. It's not like watching a TV show. I don't want you to get hurt."

"Aww...shucks, Miss...I mean, Mama Shelly, do ya mind iffen I ask him?"

"It's 'May I ask him, please,' you mean. Sure, but don't go getting your hopes up."

They finished their errands and made it back to the apartment with an hour to spare before Mr. Beaufort was to meet them. Curly pulled in just as they were walking up to the porch. Stopping to give Shelly's dog, Max, a shoulder scratch, he asked, "Who's gonna watch this fella and Garfield?"

"I called Brittany before you came over this morning, and she was thrilled to help Nicole out and earn a few extra bucks so she can buy some more *Nancy Drew* books. She is going to come over each day and play with them and make sure that they have food and water."

"'Member how she gave y'all that big break in Miss...ugh!" Tucker smacked his forehead before continuing, "I mean...Mama Shelly's kidnapping? Too bad she ain't gonna go with us. She coulda helped us."

"Help *us?*" Curly raised his eyebrows and looked over at Shelly. At her shrug, he looked back at Tucker.

Tucker took a deep breath and started talking as fast as he could. "She said that I could ask ya 'bout my helping y'all. Please? It would be so cool! I promise that I'll only do what ya tell me! Come on, please?"

Curly scratched the back of his head, laughed, and replied, "I could use a good partner, but you have to promise me that you'll not do anything without asking first. This is a very dangerous situation. Do we have us a deal?"

"Deal! Awesome! Told ya he'd let me! Wait'll I tell Cody!" Tucker raced into the house to call his best friend with the news.

Curly looked at a shocked Shelly and said, "Don't worry. I won't let him get hurt. Come on, let's go double-check and make sure we have everything finished." Curly held the front door open for her as they walked into her den.

The hour flew swiftly, and Mr. Beaufort was there to take them to the airport before they even realized it was time. They spent the drive going over all the details for getting from the airport in San Pedro to the cruise ship in Costa Maya. Once they were on the airport property, Mr. Beaufort drove them around to a hangar in the back. He pulled into the hangar next to a jet with his company's logo on the side. Once they had all the luggage on the plane, Mr. Beaufort turned to Curly and shook his hand. "I had to call in several favors to get you onboard as an investigator, so please do whatever you can to get my son back home. I can't tell you how much his mother and I appreciate all your help with this. You need anything, do not hesitate to give me a call. I'll help in any way I can."

"Sure, Mr. Beaufort. We'll do all we can to get them back here. We're also placing ourselves and Tim and Nicole in God's hands, and He's never let me down yet. We'll call you once we're onboard."

"Thank you. Hope you have a good flight. You'll enjoy flying in this jet. It's very luxurious. Good-bye. I'll be waiting for your call."

Curly, Shelly, and Tucker walked up the portable steps and entered the jet to discover six leather recliners. Once seated, Curly looked over at Shelly and Tucker and grinned, "Well, here we go! You ready to be thrust into another adventure?"

Chapter 12

After they had landed in San Pedro, they discovered that Mr. Beaufort had arranged for a limo to shuttle them the six miles over to Costa Maya and to the ship's port. When the limo arrived at the ship's entrance, they were overwhelmed at the magnitude of the ship's size. "Wow! This is one big boat!" Tucker exclaimed.

"Yeah, it is, but you'd better be sure to call it a ship. Look, I see the captain coming our way. See? That's them on that golf cart," Curly answered as they stood by their luggage next to the limo.

The captain and two other officers parked the cart and approached Curly. The captain stretched out his hand and asked, "Detective Greg Rogers?"

Curly shook his hand and replied, "Yes, sir. I'm Detective Rogers. This is my girlfriend, Shelly Gale, who is also Nicole Beaufort's best friend. And this is her...um...son, Tucker Gale."

"Glad to see you arrived safely. Just leave your luggage here. These men will make sure it makes it to your rooms. May I see your passports first? I can't let you onboard until I've checked them." They handed their passports over and watched as the captain wrote something on a form. "I thought you said your son is Tucker Gale. This passport says Tucker Irvin?" The captain looked to Curly for an explanation.

"Oh, excuse me. Here are his adoption papers. He was just officially adopted by Miss Gale yesterday as you can see. He was Tucker Irvin, but his name is now Tucker Gale. However, there hasn't been time to have his passport officially changed."

After giving the documents a thorough examination, he stepped aside and said, "Detective, due to you being an officer of the law, I am allowing you to carry your firearm while onboard. I just require that you make sure it is locked up in the security office whenever you are enjoying the ship and not investigating." At Curly's word of agreement, the Captain continued, "You may enter the ship. If you'll follow me, I'd be honored to escort you to your cabins." As they followed the captain to the ship, he continued, "Detective, our ship's head of security, Mr. Ortega, will meet you in your room in an hour to discuss the details of these unfortunate deaths with you. Here we are. Detective, you'll be staying in this cabin." Curly stepped in to find that he had been given a suite complete with hardwood floors, plasma television, king bed, and even a whirlpool bathtub.

"Miss Gale, you and Tucker will be staying directly across the corridor. I'll open it for you and leave your key card on the desk. Mr. Beaufort also purchased what we call 'fun cards' for each of you. These will allow you to get a soda, water, or coffee anytime. Here's yours, Curly, and I've left the other with your key, Miss Gale. You will need to go by the office to get your ship ID card, which you will use for purchases. We need to take your picture to put on it. Again, thank you for your help in this matter, Detective. If you need anything, just ask your steward, Juan, to give me a message. He knows to contact me immediately if you ask. Well, I'll leave you to unpack and get settled."

"Thank you for everything, sir," Curly answered as the captain exited his cabin. He then turned to Shelly and said, "Wow! This is nice! I almost feel bad that we have better accommodations than the honeymooners, but nah! Let's go look at your cabin." They crossed the hall and found the door unlocked just as the captain had said it would be. Shelly pushed it open to discover they had been given a suite just like Curly's, except for two double beds instead of a king bed.

"This is so cool!" Tucker exclaimed as he ran to open the balcony door. "Come looka here at this view!"

"Tucker, you go ahead and explore the room. I better call Nicole and let her know that we've arrived," Shelly said as she rummaged in her pocketbook looking for her phone. "Oh, there it is." Shelly punched in Nicole's number and, when she answered, said, "Hello, Mrs. Beaufort."

"Shell! Are you finally here?" Nicole shrieked. Curly had to laugh when he could even hear the shrieking from across the room.

Laughing, Shelly responded, "Yes! Why don't you come over to my cabin? It's cabin number 7294. 'Cause if I tried to find you on this huge thing, I'd be lost in a second. Oh, I better warn you. Your father-in- law arranged for Curly and me to each have a suite. I know you all are staying in a balcony room, and I feel really weird knowing we are staying in nicer cabins."

"Oh, Shell! Like I would be worried about that in the middle of this huge mess. I'm just thrilled that you and Curly are here to help us. We'll be there in just a few minutes because we are actually on the same deck! Wow, I just can't believe you are really here!"

After ending the call, Shelly turned to Curly and said, "They're on their way now. Can you believe that Mr. Beaufort arranged such nice suites for each of us? And that's after flying us down here."

"I'm really impressed too. Obviously, he's doing very well financially. Tim's fortunate to have a father that could arrange all of this for him. So, what do y'all—" Curly was interrupted by a knock on the door. Thinking Tim and Nicole had arrived, he threw the door open while yelling, "You two get yourselves in here...oh! You're not Tim and Nicole." Curly's face turned a deep red when he realized a strange man was at the door.

Chuckling, the man answered, "No, sir, I'm not. I am Juan, your steward. I wanted to stop by and introduce myself and to tell you that if you need me, just press eight on the phone. Also, your evening mealtime will be at six o'clock each evening. The captain has offered an open invitation for all three of you to sit at his table anytime, although, of course, he does understand if you desire to sit with your friends. Is there anything that I can do for you right now?"

Curly answered, "No, but thank you. Tell the captain that we'll sit with our friends this evening, but we'll be sure to sit at his table soon. Oh, there are our friends! Thank you, Juan, for the information."

Nicole and Tim entered the open door as Juan replied, "Don't forget, number eight for Juan! Have a good day." When Juan had left the cabin, Nicole ran over and gave Shelly a huge hug.

"Oh, I can't tell y'all how glad we are to see you!"

"Nicole, Tim, we would never have sent you on this cruise if we would have known the trouble you'd manage to find. We were hoping you'd have a relaxed, happy week," Shelly said as she motioned for everyone to be seated.

"Man! Look at this room, hon! Your dad got them a suite. This is so roomy and luxurious! Wait! I thought Tucker was allowed to come. Where is he?" Nicole asked as her eyes searched the room.

"Oh, he's out on the balcony probably looking for dolphins or sharks. Now have y'all had any fun at all despite these deaths?" Shelly inquired.

The two couples spent several minutes waiting for Mr. Ortega to arrive, catching up on all that the newlyweds had experienced on the ship and on their stops at the different countries they'd been to so far. When Tim was giving Curly a play-by-play account of their ping-pong game, there was another brisk knock on the door.

Shelly went and opened it to find a serious-looking official standing on the other side. "Miss Gale?" he asked in a deep voice.

"Yes, may I help you?"

"Hello, I'm Mr. Ortega, the ship's head security officer. I'm looking for a Detective Greg Rogers. By any chance, is he in here? I tried his cabin but received no answer."

"Yes, sir, he is. Come in, please." Shelly stepped back to allow him to enter.

When he spotted Nicole and Tim, he bent his head and said, "Good afternoon, Mr. and Mrs. Beaufort." Turning toward Curly, he continued, "And you must be Detective Rogers since you're the only gentleman I haven't met." The officer stretched out his hand in greeting.

Curly stood, shook his hand, and replied, "Nice to meet you, Mr. Ortega."

"Same here. Is there somewhere we can meet privately to discuss some things."

"Sure, let's go to my cabin. Shell, I'll give you a call when we've finished."

As soon as the door shut behind the two men, Shelly went and opened the sliding glass door to the balcony. "Tucker, would you please come inside for a minute?"

Once Tucker was inside and seated, Shelly said, "We need to pray. Tim, why don't you begin?"

Chapter 13

"Mr. Ortega, please would you have a seat? And may I get you some water or soda? Tim's father made sure that this fridge was well stocked," Curly said as he motioned for the security officer over to the dark burgundy love seat.

"No, thank you, Mr. Rogers. And please, it is just Ortega. That is what everyone calls me.

"Sure, Ortega, and please call me Greg, or even by my nickname Curly. I agree that it would be easier since we'll be talking quite a bit. Before you begin, please let me say that I have no intention of taking over your case or getting in your way. Tim's father, Mr. Beaufort, as well as Shelly and I, are very concerned with these deaths that have taken place here onboard the ship. We know that Tim would never take someone else's life, and Mr. Beaufort has asked me to come here to look into things. I would like it very much if I could work with you, and I intend to give any and all information that I may find to you." Curly settled back into the recliner as he waited for the officer's reply.

"Thank you for saying that. I must say that this is all highly unusual, and normally I would never tolerate an outsider taking part in an open case. However, Mr. Beaufort has a lot of pull with our company, and I've been ordered by the captain to not only give you information but to also allow you to help and assist in any way possible. I will say that I feel better after I spent some time online and pulled your file and read your background. You seem to be an honorable and respectable man, and I will value any input that you, as a detective, may be able to give me."

"That's really good of you. Would you please start at the beginning with Mitsi Craddock's death and tell me all that has taken place? I only have Tim and Nicole's account, and I know that they haven't been privy to all of the details."

"Sure, actually, I brought along a copy of my notes and the case files. I figure that would be the best way to bring you up to date. As you will see, your friend has admitted to handing the motion sickness patch that was responsible for Mitsi's death directly to her. The other victim, Barry Schmidt, died from the same poison."

"Excuse me for interrupting, but Tim never told me how the poison was given to Barry. I assume it was also through a motion sickness patch?"

Sighing, Ortega leaned back in the love seat before replying, "No, this time it was administered with a needle. While Barry was waiting for his masseuse to begin his massage, it seems Tim slipped into the room and injected him at the base of his neck while his face was down in the table."

"What! That seems a little far-fetched to me!

I can already think of lots of problems with that theory. First, where would Tim get a needle and have you found it? Secondly, how would he know that there wasn't anyone in the room with Barry? Third, how would he even get past the reception area to the massage room? I assume that there is a lady or gentleman that people check in with when they come for their massage."

Scratching his beard, Ortega slowly answered, "Right now Tim is a person of interest due to his history with the victim, Barry. I have one of my men taking statements from all of the spa staff and am hoping to have answers to those same questions when he's finished."

Curly leaned forward and tossed the case files and notes to the coffee table before continuing, "Ortega, I understand and agree with you about having Tim on your suspect list, but it's way too early to be talking of an arrest. There are just too many unanswered questions. Have you searched the Schmidts' and the Craddocks' cabins yet? If not, I'd like to assist you with that."

"I was in the process of getting the captain's permission to do just that, but I was sidetracked by the news that you were coming onboard. I'll go find the captain now and see if I can get that permission. If he does grant it, where can I reach you?"

"I should be here or in Shelly's cabin with my friends. If we decide to go somewhere else onboard, I'll leave word with Juan, my steward," Curly answered as he walked to the door to open it for the officer.

As Ortega reached the door, Curly reached out his hand. "Thank you for agreeing to include me on this case. I know you were commanded to do it, but I still appreciate your helpful attitude. I'm looking forward to working with you."

Ortega responded with a hearty handshake before replying, "The same here. I'll be seeing you in a little while. Enjoy your afternoon."

Curly stood and watched the officer stride down the corridor before closing the door. Deciding to read over the files in hopes of finding more suspects, Curly walked over to the love seat, sat down, put his head in his hands, and sought the Lord's help. *Lord, Ortega seems determined that Tim is the one responsible. I know that there is no way Tim would commit murder, and especially while on his honeymoon. Help me find something in here that will get his attention off of Tim and onto someone else. Once again, I'm asking for your wisdom.*

Chapter 14

At the knock on her door, Shelly opened it to see Curly standing there with a half-grin and his hands in his pockets. Looking around, Shelly asked, "Where's Mr. Ortega?"

"He's getting the captain's permission to search the Schmidts' and the Craddocks' cabins. He's allowing me to read his notes and his case files, so I'm going to sit on my balcony while I read over them. I really wish I could let you read them too, but I better not let anyone else see them. Do you think y'all can find something to do this afternoon while I'm working?" Curly asked as he stepped into the cabin.

"Well, I really have no idea! Nicole? Tim? Any suggestions?" Shelly asked.

Before they could even take a breath, Tucker raced in from the balcony and shouted, "I have one! Let's go up to the waterslide! I saw a picture of it on this here brochure. It looks like totally awesome! I'll go get my swimming trunks on!" He then ran off into the bathroom to change before anyone could give him an answer.

Tim laughed, shrugged, and said, "Sounds like we're going to the waterslide. What do you two think?"

Nicole looked at her watch

and replied, "Shell, I really don't want to get all wet this close to dinner 'cause then we'd have to shower and get cleaned up. I wouldn't mind going with them and watching, though. What do you think of you and me sitting on the sidelines in one of those comfy deck chairs and chat while they do the waterslide?"

"That sounds heavenly. Curly, why don't we meet you back here at five thirty unless you need to go do those searches with Mr. Ortega? If you do, just leave me a note on the door if you aren't going to make dinner." Shelly requested.

"Oh, I'm not missing dinner! I've heard all about the delicious meals these cruise ships prepare, and I'm going to make sure that I don't miss that! I'll see you all at five thirty then. Bye for now and have fun! Oh yeah, don't forget your sunscreen!" Curly reminded as he made his way back to his cabin.

Tucker came running out of the bathroom and started jumping up and down with impatience. "Come on, y'all! What's takin' so long?"

"Okay, buddy, slow down a little. We're going already! Shell, Nicky and I will meet you two at the waterslide in fifteen minutes. We need to run up to our cabin and grab some things. If you beat us there, be sure and save us some chairs in the shade. Oh, and Tucker? Be sure to make yourself an ice cream cone. The ice cream station is self-serve, and it's right next to the pool area."

"Cool! Come on, Mama Shelly, let's go!" Tucker shouted as he ran to the door, "Oh, almost forgot my goggles! Okay, now I'm ready!"

Rolling her eyes while winking at Nicole, Shelly laughed as she answered, "All right! I'm ready. We'll see you two in fifteen minutes, if not sooner."

A little more than fifteen minutes later, Nicole and Tim finally spotted Tucker's bright red hair in the line for the waterslide. "Tim, I had no idea it'd be so crowded! I hope we can find Shelly."

"Just look for that white floppy hat and those humongous pink sunglasses that she was wearing. Oh, I see her. Look, she's waving a towel to get our attention! Go enjoy your girl time while I try get some energy out of Tucker," suggested Tim as he bent to give her a quick kiss on the tip of her nose.

"Okay. Have fun and remember to smile 'cause I brought the camera with me," reminded Nicole as she watched her husband walk over to the slide area. Walking toward Shelly, she shouted, "Shell, you want a soda before I sit down?"

"I already got one for each of us while I was waiting. We were here within five minutes 'cause Tucker was so excited!" Shelly patted the deck lounger next to her and continued, "Come on, just sit and relax."

They spent the afternoon catching up on all that had been going on and talking over the case. Shelly tried to reassure her that she didn't need to be worried about Tim being arrested, but Nicole would just shrug and say, "I know, but it's so hard to not worry. I just can't believe this is all happening on my, I mean, our honeymoon!" Shelly then reminded her that everyone back home in Pilotview was praying for them and that none of this was taking God by surprise. Just as she finished giving Nicole a quick encouraging hug, Maggy and Luke Tolson walked by and stopped when they saw Nicole.

"Hi, Nicole! Where's that handsome husband of yours? I wouldn't have thought anyone would be able to tear him away from you after seeing how he looked at you!" Maggy asked as she sat on the edge of the chair next to Nicole.

"Oh, hey, Maggy. He's on the waterslide with a friend of ours. By the way, this is my best friend, Shelly Gale. Shelly, this is the couple that we played ping- pong with the other day, Maggy and Luke Tolson."

"Nice to meet you, Maggy and Luke. I heard the guys beat you two gals pretty badly!" Shelly responded while shaking their hands.

Laughing, Maggy answered, "Yeah, but no big deal. Best friends, huh? Wow! I can't believe you brought friends with you on your honeymoon, Nicole! Wait a minute, I don't think that we've seen you onboard, but then it is a big ship..." Maggy let her voice trail off as she looked at Shelly quizzically.

Shelly just laughed and replied, "Yes, it is a big ship. What do y'all think of the cruise so far?"

Maggy shuddered and looked at Luke before responding, "Well, it'd be a lot better if it weren't for those two people dying. Oh yeah, guess what we heard? Nicole, we heard talk that they're going to arrest Tim! Is that true?"

Seeing her friend's face go pale at the mention of Tim being arrested, Shelly jumped in before Nicole could answer, "Nonsense! Why, anyone who knows Tim knows that he could never hurt anyone, let alone kill them! People should make sure they have all of the facts before spreading such vicious lies!" Furious, Shelly stood to her feet and motioned to Nicole. "Come on, Nicky, I say it's past time to find your hubby and my boy and go get ready for dinner. Nice meeting you, folks."

As they picked up their things to make their way to Tim and Tucker, they heard a loud piercing squeal followed by a lady's voice shouting, "No! No! He can't be dead! Someone help me!"

Chapter 15

As Curly read and reread over the officer's notes and case files, he started jotting down any leads and questions that he had. Being a methodical person, he started one of his many lists.

Nicole said that Mitsi and Mark are from Michigan, but Mark's address has them listed in New York. Why the difference?

How did Tim get a needle? Where is the needle?

How did Tim get past the receptionist?

How did Tim know Barry would be alone?

Why would Tim kill Mitsi when he just met her?

Curly realized after he finished reading through the files again that Tim was the only link so far that had connections with both victims. *No wonder Officer Ortega has him at the top of his list. Surely on a ship this large that has so many activities, these two victims had to have crossed paths with other people who knew both of them. Wait! That gives me an idea! Maybe they all eat at the same table?*

 He picked up the cabin phone and dialed his steward, Juan. "Juan, how are you? Would you please tell me how I can reach the dining room? I need to find out when and where the two victims sat for dinner. The

captain told me that you would be able to help with anything I needed. Can you get that for me? You can get me a seating chart? Wonderful! How long before you can have it? Great! I'll see you in thirty minutes." After hanging up with Juan, Curly realized that Tim and Nicole might also be able to give him the same information, especially if Barry and Mitsi had dined with them. *Guess I'll go track them down at the waterslide. I sure hope Shell has been able to encourage Nicole some this afternoon. She was looking like this investigation was beginning to wear on her.*

Curly found himself whistling that old comforting hymn, "Does Jesus Care?" while walking toward the elevators. *That's interesting. Why is it that I always seem to whistle the older hymns and never the new church songs? Seems like those older hymns are just easier to whistle, and they have such great messages. I'm so glad that Jesus does care about this situation Tim is in.* Reaching the elevators, Curly had just pushed the Up button when the doors slid open to reveal, to his surprise, Tim, Nicole, Shelly, and Tucker. "Well, lookey here! How did y'all know that I was coming to look for you?"

"So you've already heard?" Shelly asked as they stepped off the elevator.

"Heard what? I was just coming to find y'all to ask Tim and Nicole something. Hey! Have you been crying? What's going on, Shell?" Curly asked quietly after noticing the strain on all their faces.

"Oh, Curly! Someone else has died!" Nicole blurted out before Shelly could respond.

"What! Who? When!" demanded Curly.

"Not here, Curly, let's all go to my cabin so we can have some privacy," Shelly said as they turned to go toward her door.

Curly reached for Shelly's hand as they walked down the narrow corridor. "Do you have the key card?" he asked as they approached the cabin.

"She gave it to me, Curly. I'll git it fer y'all." Tucker raced ahead of the group and had the door open by the time the rest of them reached it.

After everyone sat down and got comfortable, Curly turned to Tim and inquired, "Okay, what happened?"

Running his hand through his short blond hair, Tim stammered, "I wish I knew. Tucker and I were having a blast on the waterslide when all of a sudden we heard a lady screaming and hollering. When we looked to see what was going on, we saw people rushing over toward the grill station, so I hollered for Tucker to come with me, and we ran to find the ladies. They had also heard the screaming, only they actually heard the lady scream, 'No, he can't be dead! Someone help me!' So we all rushed over to see what was going on. By that time, the ship's doctor was leaning over a man's body examining him. When he looked up to tell the lady who was screaming that the man was dead, I about fainted myself. You're never going to believe who it was, Curly!"

"Who? Don't tell me that you knew him too?" Curly demanded.

Laughing nervously, Tim continued, "Ah, yes, you could say that I knew him. It's our waiter that we have every night for dinner...Ramone! Can you believe I know all three of the people who have died? Would someone please tell me what's going on? Why on earth would someone want to make my life miserable? What have I done to cause someone to hate me so much to see me arrested?" Tim slammed his fist into the pillow on the love seat before pulling Nicole into a hug. "Honey, I am so sorry about all of this. I promise you that I'm going to take you on another honeymoon to make up for this one," he said. He then leaned forward and put his head into his hands, moaning.

"Oh, Tim! I'm not worried about that! I'm just so afraid that security officer is going to arrest you since you're connected to all three victims! I can't stand the thought of them putting you in jail!" Nicole answered as she rubbed his shoulders.

"Listen, you two, don't give up yet. We know it's not Tim, so let's get busy thinking of other people who knew all three of them. Did Ramone wait on Mitsi and Barry also?" Curly inquired.

Tim turned and looked at Nicole over his shoulder before answering, "Well, yes, and I don't know. Yes, he waited on Mitsi because she sat at our table. We have no idea if he waited on Barry because Barry wasn't assigned to our table, but he could've been assigned to Ramone's table for the late dinnertime. We have no idea."

"Well Juan, my steward is getting that information for me right now." Hearing a knock on the door, he continued, "That's probably him right now." Curly walked over and opened the door expecting to see his steward but was surprised to see the security officer at the door. "Oh! Hello, Ortega, come on in."

"Greg, is Tim Beaufort in there? I'm looking for him," Ortega announced to a stunned cabin.

Chapter 16

"Please come in, Ortega. May I get you a soda or water?" Curly asked.

"No, thank you. I'm here to question Mr. Beaufort about another death we've had, but I'll need to question him privately. Mr. Beaufort, could we please go to your cabin?"

Before Tim could answer, Shelly jumped to her feet and said, "Come on, everyone, let's head over to my cabin and give them their privacy." As everyone began gathering up all their belongings, Curly motioned with his head for Shelly to meet him in the corridor.

"Shell, y'all go ahead and get cleaned up and ready for dinner. I'm going to stay here with Tim in case he needs me." Taking her chin in his hand, he continued, "Try not to worry, okay? I'm positive that he doesn't have enough to retain him."

"Whew! I should hope not! We'll stay in either my cabin or Nicky's until we hear from you then. We're praying for both of you." She squeezed his hand before following the others into her cabin.

After Curly shut the door to his own cabin, Ortega began talking. "Mr. Beaufort, we've had another suspicious death onboard our ship. Since you've had history with the other two victims, I have several questions that I must ask."

"Do I need a lawyer present? And I want Curly to stay and listen, please."

"You may have a lawyer if you wish. That's entirely up to you, but I'm not here to arrest you. Do you want a lawyer? If so, I'll have the captain see if he can locate one onboard."

Looking to Curly for direction before answering, Tim responded, "No, not yet. Go ahead with your questions. I've got nothing to hide."

"The gentleman who died today is Ramone Rodriguez, a staff member of our cruise line. Do you know Mr. Rodriguez?"

"Yes, but not very well. He is, I mean was, our waiter and a really awesome waiter at that. He did an outstanding job of anticipating our needs and wants before we could even ask. But other than placing my order or thanking him, I've never had a conversation with him or seen him at any other time."

"Very well. Have you ever been to the country of Honduras?"

Giving a short laugh, Tim sheepishly answered, "Um, no. I don't even think I could point to it on a map!

"Where have you been since I left all of you earlier this afternoon? And have you been with anyone during this time?"

"Well, I was with my wife, Nicole, and Shelly, Tucker, and Curly here for a little while until Tucker and I decided to go to the waterslide. Nicole and I went to our cabin to change and get our stuff and then met Shelly and Tucker at the slide about fifteen minutes later. After that? I was with Tucker and at least a couple of hundred other folks at the waterslide. I was having so much fun with Tucker that I didn't even see that Ramone was in the area, although I don't even know if I'd recognize him without his waiter's uniform on. Anyway, I was with Tucker at the slide until we heard a lady screaming."

"For the fifteen to twenty minutes that you and your wife were apart from the others, did anyone see you?"

"Huh? I have no clue. Let me think. Oh yes! The housekeeping lady saw us! She was just putting a towel stingray on our bed when we came in to change. She saw us! And she saw us when we left because she was at the next door getting ready to go in when we walked by, and Nicky stopped and complimented her on the towel animal."

"That's good, Mr. Beaufort, very good. Let me check on this and get back to you. Tomorrow when we get to Nassau, you're to remain on the ship unless I tell you otherwise. I've already put a restriction on your ID badge. What do you think, Greg?" Ortega turned and asked Curly as he put his notepad in his shirt pocket.

"Sounds to me like there's no way Tim could've murdered Ramone. So, it's time to start looking elsewhere. Did you get the captain's permission for those searches?"

"Yes, I was on my way to ask you to accompany me when I was given the news that Mr. Rodriguez had died. Would you like to go to the Craddocks' with me now? A word of warning, Mr. Craddock has been very understandably upset and hostile through all of this, so I'm taking another officer with me in case he doesn't want us to complete the search. Mr. Beaufort, I suggest that you go back to your cabin until dinner. Greg, let's go."

Curly held up his hand and said, "Hold on. I need to let my friends know that I might be missing dinner. Tim, go and try to enjoy this afternoon with your wife. We'll figure this out, I promise. And remember, God's still on the throne!"

Chapter 17

The inside of Shelly's cabin was extremely noisy as Tucker and Shelly were getting cleaned up and ready for the evening meal. "Remember, Tucker, no shorts or T-shirts. Wear your blue-collared shirt with your khaki pants," Shelly said as he went to take his turn in the shower.

Sighing, he replied, "Yeah, whatever."

Before he could shut the door, she stuck her head in the restroom and asked, "Excuse me? What did you say?

"Oh, sorry! I meant, 'Yes, Ma'am.' Sorry 'bout that!" Tucker corrected himself as he shrugged with a grin.

"That's what I thought you meant to say." Winking at him to let him know that she wasn't upset, she then turned to Nicole. "Nicky, do you need to go back to your cabin now? Or do you want to wait for us?"

Nicole leaned her head back on the headrest of the plush recliner, closed her eyes, and responded, "I'll wait here if you don't mind. It just feels so good to close my eyes. I have the beginning of a headache. Besides, I'd rather wait here for Tim anyway." Shuddering,

Nicole continued, "I really don't want to be alone with all these murders happening."

"I totally understand that! You just take a short catnap and try to get rid of that headache. I'm just going to go out on the balcony while Tucker is showering." Sliding open the balcony door, she stepped outside and quietly shut the door so she wouldn't disturb Nicole. She walked over to the railing and enjoyed feeling the ocean's breeze on her face as she watched the sun start to change from yellowish-orange to a dark red-orange. Just as she was going to sit down to watch the sun set, she had the thrill of seeing a pod of dolphins jump up out of the water a few feet from the ship! Laughing, she leaned over to watch them. *How awesome! It looks like they're trying to race us. Boy, Tucker is going to be disappointed that he missed this! This is such a beautiful place, Lord! I wonder how much more beautiful it would have been if Adam hadn't brought the curse of sin upon this world? When I see something as beautiful as this, I just can't help thinking how awesome heaven's going to be. Jesus, here we are again in the middle of a murder, or I should say several murder investigations. Would you please help Curly and lead him as he helps Officer Ortega? And please protect Tim, Nicole, and all of us while we're dealing with...* She wasn't finished praying but had to stop as she heard a knock on the cabin door. She quickly went to get it so Nicole would continue to rest.

She was pleasantly surprised as she opened the door to see a smiling Tim on the other side. "Is a beautiful Mrs. Beaufort in there?" he asked.

"What? I thought your mother was in Florida with your dad?" Shelly teased.

"Ha-ha, Shelly, you are so not funny!" Nicole walked up and gave her husband a big hug and a kiss. "How did the meeting go? And where's Curly?"

Tim kept his arm around her shoulder as he answered, "I'm feeling a lot better about things after today. I was either with someone or seen by others during the time Ramone died, so hopefully this'll get me off that officer's radar! I believe Curly and Officer Ortega are going to do some investigating. Come on, honey, we don't have much time. Let's go get ready for dinner. Shell, we'll call you on the ship's phone when we're headed to the dining room, okay?"

"Sure, see you in a bit." She shut the door and jumped when she turned and found Tucker standing right behind her. "Tucker! You scared me to death! I had no idea that you were behind me."

"Sorry, you probably didn't hear me 'cause you was talkin' with Tim. You know, I used to hate that guy for putting me in foster care, but I had a pretty good time with him today. Maybe he's not so bad after all!"

Shelly chuckled and replied, "I'll be sure to tell Nicole that you approve. I'm sure she'll be thrilled to hear that you now like her husband."

"Ha-ha. I've got to git good as you at usin' sarcasm! Did Tim say that Curly's investigatin'? Where's he at? Can I go help?"

Shelly put her hands on her hips and put her teacher look on as she answered, "No, young man, you are going to dinner with me. Now let's get something straight. You are a boy, and as a matter of respect, I expect you to call any adults by Mister, Missus, or Miss, understand?"

When Tucker responded with only a nod, she continued, "Excuse me? I think you meant to say something?"

Raising his one eyebrow, Tucker responded quickly, "Yes, Ma'am."

"That's better. Now I don't ever want to hear you calling an adult by his or her first name again. Oh my gracious! Look at the time! Go, quickly find a comb and see if you can get that cowlick of yours to lie down while I go put on my makeup." They quickly finished getting ready and were looking for the key card when Tim called to tell them that they'd meet them outside the dining room.

After they were able to finally get an elevator and make it to the dining room lobby, they were surprised at the number of people standing everywhere waiting on the dining room doors to open. Being only five feet and two inches, Shelly had a difficult time seeing over people as she looked for her friends. Just when she was beginning to get frustrated, she finally heard, "Shell, over here!" Turning, she saw Tim and Nicole waving at them from next to a tall green fake fern.

She and Tucker made their excuses as they worked their way through the crowd to get to them. As they walked up, Tim said, "Sorry, we just got here. I hope you weren't waiting on us long. Just as we were walking out the door, Curly called. He had tried to reach you, but you must've already left. He wanted me to pass along a message that he is coming to dinner and should only be a few minutes late. He also said that he has some good news for all of us."

Chapter 18

Shelly was very glad that she had thought to bring her camera because the dining room was decorated so beautifully with flowers and ice sculptures everywhere. She couldn't resist taking a picture of the awed expression on Tucker's face as he took it all in.

"Miss, I mean, Mama Shelly, I ain't never seen animals carved out of ice before! Lookey at that one over there! It's a mama dolphin with her baby. How on earth did they make it light up purple like that?" Tucker was so excited that he wasn't even stopping to take a breath and kept turning around, trying to see everything at once until he bumped into one of the other passengers. "Oh, 'scuse me. Sorry 'bout that!" Tucker's face and neck turned as red as his hair from being so embarrassed.

Laughing, Shelly threw her arm around him and pulled him into a half-hug next to her. "It's okay, but let's sit down before you actually knock someone over. Nicole and Tim, where's your table?"

Nicole pointed across the room to the far corner and answered, "That's where we are assigned. Tim, I wonder who'll replace Ramone? It seems wrong for us to be having fun and enjoying ourselves after what just happened a couple of hours ago."

Tim replied as he pulled her chair out for her, "Yeah, hon, I agree, but let's try to enjoy what we can. Hey, you two make sure you order the chocolate melting cake. It's out of this world! In fact, it's so good that we haven't ordered anything else for dessert all week!"

"Check out these plates! They have the same animals on them as the ice sculptures! How awesome! Rats! I got stuck with the lousy parrot! Wish I had the mama dolphin with her baby!" Tucker complained good-naturedly.

Nicole smiled at him and answered, "Well, I happen to like parrots! In fact, we saw several while eating lunch the other day at XCaret in Cozumel. Man, that feels like a lifetime ago! Anyway, I'll trade plates with you, Tucker, if you want because I have the one with the dolphins!" When she held up the plate to show him, they all started switching plates around the table. They were all laughing when their new waiter approached the table.

"Good evening, my name is Fritz, and I'll be your waiter for the rest of your vacation. I apologize for not knowing your drink preferences, but be assured that it won't happen again. These two gentlemen standing behind me are my assistants. Please let one of us know if there is anything we could do to make your meal more enjoyable. I understand that we have three new guests dining with us this evening?" Fritz raised his eyebrows as he looked around waiting for confirmation before continuing.

"Um, so far only two of us..." Shelly began but was interrupted by a voice behind her.

"No, sir, you were correct the first time. There are three of us. Allow me to introduce myself, Greg Rogers, and this is my girlfriend, Shelly Gale, and her son, Tucker. Sorry to interrupt, please continue." Curly winked at Shelly and ruffled Tucker's hair as he took the open seat next to Shelly.

Clearing his throat, Fritz continued, "Yes, well, as you know, the staff of the ship are all from different countries. I myself am from Dusseldorf, Germany, but I do speak and understand English very well. Now then, let's begin with your drink orders."

After the orders were placed and the waiters had departed to the kitchen, Shelly turned to Curly and said, "Enough suspense already! What's the good news?

"Well, first, I believe we need to get Tim to introduce us to our dining companions. We don't want to be rude, do we?" Curly smiled as he looked over at Tim to take the lead.

"I'd be glad to, Curly. The couple on your right is Candy and Victor Anderson. They're from Georgia and go on a cruise every year." Tim paused to give them time to shake hands and exchange hellos before continuing, "On my right are the Mains from South Carolina. Becky's a retired kindergarten teacher, Shelly. She and Nicky have become great friends. And the empty seat is where Mark Craddock should be sitting, although without his wife." Tim shrugged and went on. "He's probably just grabbing a bite from the buffet."

After they had exchanged pleasantries with their new friends, Shelly turned to Curly and spoke quietly. "If you make me wait much longer, Buster, I might just have to sic my big brother, Marcus, on you! Out with this good news already!"

Laughing, Curly leaned back and stretched out his legs under the table as he replied, "Oh no! Not Marcus! I'm so scared!" Chuckling at Shelly's facial expression, he continued, "Okay, I'll have mercy on you. Let me start with the searches. Officer Ortega and I searched the Craddocks' and the Schmidts' cabins. At first look, we didn't find much, but Officer Ortega did take a lot of papers into evidence to examine later. As we were searching the Craddocks' cabin, I suggested that we also search Tim and Nicole's also, which we're going to do after dinner's over."

Shelly gasped and interrupted. "That doesn't sound much like good news to me!"

"Yeah, to us either! Search our cabin? Doesn't he need a warrant?" Tim demanded.

"I'm getting to the good news, and no, he doesn't, Tim. Since the ship is the property of the cruise line, all he needs is the captain's permission. Don't worry! It won't be a problem, right?" At Tim's nod, Curly continued, "Well, I got Ortega talking about how Tim couldn't have murdered Ramone, and after some rules were agreed to, he's granting Tim permission to go onshore and off the ship tomorrow."

"Really? Wow! That's terrific! Wait, did you say rules? What sort of rules did you agree to?" Tim inquired.

Sighing, Curly replied, "Since I'm an officer of the law, he's agreed to allow you to go off the ship only if you agree to stay with me and in my sight at all times. I promised him and gave him my word that you would be with me at all times. Can you deal with that?"

Tim put his hand out for Curly to shake and enthusiastically responded, "Deal! That is good news! This must mean that he doesn't think I killed anyone!" Tim looked at Nicole with a huge grin on his face.

"Whoa, slow down a little. You're still considered a person of interest, and until he or we have these murders figured out, he's not about to cross you off his list. At least, you can enjoy your day tomorrow!"

Chapter 19

After the scrumptious dinner, they all decided to go play tennis on the upper deck while Curly and Officer Ortega searched Tim and Nicole's cabin. Curly pulled Shelly aside as they waited for the elevator and asked her if she'd like to go on a moonlight walk with him around the ship's deck to watch the night sky after he was finished searching the cabin. When she quickly agreed with a smile, he made his exit and went to the security office to meet up with Ortega. He entered the cramped space to see Ortega eating his meal while reading a file.

Looking up at Curly's short rap on the open door, Ortega smiled and said, "Come in and have a seat. I'm almost finished eating. While I eat, why don't you read over Ramone's file? It seems he died by the same poison as our other two victims."

"Really? It'd be quicker if you just gave me the highlights."

"Sure. Seems the doc thinks the poison was given through either food or drink this time. I really need a break in this case! In just two days, we'll be back in port, and the FBI will be wanting to take it over. I would really like to have it all wrapped up by then."

"I understand. I'm going to do all I can to help you do just that. I never did hear what your men found out at the spa."

"Oh yes, well, they showed the receptionist Tim's photograph, but she states that she's never seen him. We went through their computer records of all logins, and it was all just the usual."

"The usual?"

"Yes, you know, the different masseuses, barbers, hairstylists, housekeeping, pharmacy deliveries, maintenance workers, deli deliveries, etcetera. Lots of people were there, and every one of them had a legitimate reason."

"Maybe someone was disguised as maintenance or housekeeping?" Curly suggested.

Officer Ortega scratched his chin, stood to his feet, and threw his Styrofoam container away before replying, "Maybe. Later this evening I'm going to be studying the security footage from the receptionist area. I hope to spot someone who doesn't match their photograph that's in the ship's database." Wiping his hands with a napkin, he went on, "Let's go search Mr. Beaufort's cabin. I have one of my men searching Ramone's cabin as well. Maybe between the two of us we'll get a lucky break."

Curly followed the officer as he took the elevator and back corridors that were reserved for the staff to use and was amazed to see how quickly they reached the door. As Ortega opened it with his master key, Curly sent a quick plea to heaven, *Please help this to be a huge waste of our time, Lord. Help us to figure this out soon.*

The two men decided to search side-by-side as they had the other cabins and started at the closet. Curly had conducted a multitude of searches during his career as a detective, but this search made him feel strange. He didn't enjoy going through his friends' personal possessions. Curly was thankful when they discovered that the closet only held the typical assortment of clothing, shoes, belts, etc., so they moved over to the desk.

Before starting on the desk, Ortega noted, "Hmm...no laptop? Surely in this day of instant communication, he would've brought one. Wonder where it is?"

"Ortega, remember, they are on their honeymoon. I was with them when they were loading their stuff into the limo to leave for the airport, and I don't recall seeing either one of them with a laptop." Having cleared up that issue, they began searching again. They pulled every drawer out and searched every crevice, but once again, there was nothing. Seeing the small safe in the wall above the desk, Curly offered to open it since Tim had given him the code.

"Go ahead and use the code he gave you. If it doesn't work, the captain and I both have override codes to access any safe," Ortega commented as he watched Greg successfully use the code Tim had given him. Inside, they found only passports and wallets as Tim had told him would be there. The room itself was next, but it also had nothing out of the ordinary. The only place left was the extremely small bathroom.

"How do you want to do this? There's no way both of us will fit in there at the same time while conducting a search," Curly asked.

"You stand in the doorway and watch. I'll do the searching," Ortega replied as he pulled the shower door open. Curly watched closely as Ortega opened every bottle and looked in it. Next, Ortega searched the toilet but found nothing there either. When he reached the counter-top, Curly groaned because of the overwhelming number of nail polish bottles, perfume bottles, makeup, lotions, and prescription bottles that Nicole and Tim had with them.

"Ortega, why don't I help you look through those so we can get out of here sometime this evening? Just hand a few of them over here to me. Nicky sure does love to polish her nails!"

Ortega whistled as he saw Curly's point. "That's a lot of nail polish. Sure, here, take this handful and get busy while I take a look underneath the sink."

Curly began to wish he had brought nose clips with him as he began opening bottle after bottle. He just knew he was going to get a headache after smelling all those fumes from the polishes. As he was struggling to open the third one that was stuck, he was distracted by a noise from Ortega. "Something wrong?"

"Greg, we have a problem," Ortega replied as he knelt on the floor looking under the sink.

"What's wrong? A broken pipe?"

"No, you'd better come and see for yourself while I go and get my camera."

Curly bent down and was dismayed to see a syringe duct-taped to the underside of the counter.

Chapter 20

Tim and Nicole's moods had improved tremendously after Curly had told them that Tim was going to be allowed to go into Nassau the next day. The tennis games were filled with teasing, laughter, and a lot of good-natured trash talking.

As they were finishing up their fourth match, Curly walked up with a somber look on his face and stood watching their banter. Seeing him standing there, Shelly walked up to him and quietly asked, "Curly? What is it? You look upset about something."

Raking his fingers through his hair, Curly blew out a huge sigh before answering, "Yeah, you could say that I'm upset. Hold on, though, 'cause I want Tim and Nicole to hear my news." Turning to the newlyweds hugging each other out on the court, Curly raised his voice and called out, "Could you two come over here a minute? I need to tell you something." Once they were close, he looked around to make sure they were alone before continuing, "Listen, I'm afraid I have some awful news, but before I share it, I want all of you to promise that you'll let me completely finish before asking any questions. Can you promise me that?" After each of them had nodded, Curly began to say, "Okay, the bad news is that Officer Ortega and I found a syringe taped under the counter of your bathroom sink, Tim, and both of us are pretty certain it will prove to have the same poison in it that's been responsible for all three deaths." He paused as they all gasped and appreciated that they didn't ask any questions.

He went on, "Both Ortega and I also believe that it's a plant and that someone is trying to frame you, Tim. We feel this way for a couple of reasons. Our first reason is because there were no prints on the syringe, and the second is because you were seen by people all afternoon and couldn't have murdered Ramone. If the syringe were yours and you were trying to hide it in your bathroom, then your prints would've been all over it. So, Officer Ortega and I have come up with a plan to try and draw the killer out. The killer is obviously trying to get you arrested, Tim, so that's what we're going to do. Wait! Let me finish, please. Officer Ortega is going to be here in just a few minutes, so I need to quickly fill you in. Like I said, he's coming in a few minutes and is going to very publicly arrest Tim and walk him through as many public areas as possible on his way back to the security office with the hopes of the killer seeing you. Now, Tim, we all know that this won't be a real arrest. It's just a show for the killer. We're hoping he'll relax and do something really stupid to give himself away. Now let's all play some tennis and act like we're having the best time of our lives. Be sure to act outraged and surprised when Ortega shows up. I know this sounds crazy, but can all of you do this?"

Tim whistled and said, "Wow! The syringe was in our cabin! Man, I am so thankful that you're here to work on this with Officer Ortega. Sure, I can put on a good act. Won't be too hard because I still remember how I felt when Ortega was seriously considering me. Let's get to it."

The two couples quickly split up into two teams and had Tucker to be the line judge. The match had just gotten underway when the officer approached with two other men following behind him.

"Excuse me for interrupting what looks to be an enjoyable game, but, Mr. Beaufort, may I please have a word with you a moment?" After Tim had walked over to the officer, Mr. Ortega raised his voice and loudly said, "Mr. Beaufort, we are taking you into custody for the murders of Mitsi Craddock, Barry Schmidt, and Ramone Rodriguez until we reach port in Florida. Once there we will be turning you and this investigation over to the FBI. Would you like us to find a legal representative for you?" Ortega asked as he motioned to one of his men, who quickly stepped behind Tim and cuffed his hands behind his back.

"Wait a minute! You can't arrest my husband! I know he would never murder anyone! This is ridiculous! Curly, please, do something to stop this!" Nicole pleaded as she started crying.

Shaking his head, Curly responded, "Wish I could, Nicole, but I have no authority here. May I go with you, Officer?"

"No, you may not. I'll be conducting an interrogation with him privately in the security office. You may come see him later this evening after I have finished." Ortega then pulled Tim by the elbow and led him off to the elevators with the two men following silently behind.

Watching them go, Nicole continued her playacting by letting out a shriek and yelling, "Oh, Shell! What am I gonna do?"

Shelly pulled her into a hug and patted her on the back. "Shh! It'll be okay. Why don't we go to my cabin?"

"I agree. That's a wonderful suggestion. Let's get away from all of these people. Come on, ladies, let's go," Curly said as he put his arm around Shelly's shoulders.

Once they were in Shelly's cabin, Curly picked up the phone and called Ortega to arrange a time for them to visit Tim. After hanging up, Curly turned to them and informed them that they were going to visit Tim at midnight.

"Midnight! Why so late?" Shelly asked as she took a Diet Coke from the small refrigerator.

"It's already ten, and that'll give him time with Tim for the fake interrogation. By the way, y'all did a marvelous acting job. If I hadn't known better, I would have thought Nicole was really upset! So what do y'all want to do while waiting?"

Nicole yawned, stretched out on the sofa, and replied, "Thank you for the compliment, Curly. It wasn't hard to act upset because I've been close to it for a couple of days now. If y'all don't mind, I'm gonna catch a quick nap. I'm exhausted! What do y'all want to do?"

"Hmm...I'm not the least bit tired after playing that tennis game, but Tucker should be heading toward bed soon. Guess I'll read or watch TV in the other room. You, Curly?"

"Well, since you're not tired, what would you say to you and me taking that stroll along the deck and go look at the stars, Shell? Tucker'll be fine as long as Nicole's here."

"Oh, what a lovely idea! Let's do it! I mean, if it's okay with you, Nicole?"

Nicole assured them that she and Tucker would be fine and would enjoy the quiet, so Shelly and Curly said their good night to Tucker and headed out for their walk. As they left the cabin, Curly reached out for Shelly's hand and said, "Come on, Shell, there's this awesome view from the back, I mean the stern, of the ship on the Sky Deck."

When they finally made it to the Sky Deck, Curly pulled Shelly close and whispered, "Isn't this just beautiful?"

"Oh, Curly, it really is! Look at all of those stars and the moon's reflection in the water! This is just so romantic. Thank you for bringing me up here. I've got to tell you, I'm so glad that I know Tim's arrest is a fake, or I would never be able to enjoy a moment of this."

"Me too, me too. You know, Shell, as soon as I knew we were coming to this cruise to help Tim and Nicole, I realized that I didn't want to waste this marvelous opportunity that God has put in my lap."

"Huh? What are you talking about? What opportunity?"

"This opportunity." Curly took one of Shelly's hands as he reached into his pocket, pulled out a diamond ring, and knelt on one knee. Totally enjoying the look of shock on Shelly's face, he softly continued, "Shelly, God brought us together in a very unusual way, but right from the start, I knew that there was something special about you. As we've gotten to be friends and have been dating these last several months, I've come to love the lady that you are. You are so beautiful inside and out. I love your caring and compassionate way with others, but I mostly love how you live for the Lord. I can't imagine not having you by my side for the rest of my life. So, Shelly, would you do me the honor of agreeing to be my wife?"

Chapter 21

Shelly squealed as she threw her arms around Curly's neck. "Yes! Of course, yes! I can't believe you've had a ring with you this whole time! It's absolutely stunning! Oh, Curly, look at it sparkling in the moonlight!"

Curly chuckled and gave her a big squeeze as he touched his forehead to hers so that he could look into her brown eyes. "I have to say, I'm relieved to see you so excited. Now hold on to your hat because I have another big question. We've been through many things together and have spent quite a while dating, so I am confident that I know the real you. What I'm trying to say here, and doing it rather badly, is... what do you think about us getting married on our last day at sea?"

"What! Curly? Are you serious?"

"You bet I am! I don't want to wait any longer to have you as my wife. Now I've had the advantage of knowing that I was going to do this, so I've done a lot of thinking. I know that you would want your family to be here for this special day, and I wish Chad could be here as well. I don't think we could manage to get them all here onboard in time, but we could set up a webcam for the ceremony and use Skype so that they can watch the wedding live on their computers. Then when we get home, we could plan a huge reception in a week or so. I know I haven't given you much time to think about it, but—"

Before he could say any more, Shelly interrupted. "I think it sounds perfect! A wedding at sea? Wow! It doesn't get any more romantic than that! What am I saying? I now have a lot to do tomorrow! I have to get a dress, flowers, a cake, ugh! I'm so glad Nicole's here to help me. She's going to be so excited!"

"Really? You're all for it? I can't believe it! That means in just two days we'll be Mr. and Mrs. Greg Rogers! Oh, Shelly! You know what I'm thinking? I'm thinking about how God's taken something that's pretty awful, these murders, and is bringing something really good out of it. I love you so much, honey. I think we should head back and ask Tucker what he thinks and show Nicole your ring."

The beaming couple practically ran back to the cabin and were laughing and giggling as they approached the door. Shelly put a finger to her lips, quietly unlocked the door, and then tiptoed over to Nicole, who was sleeping so soundly that she was drooling on the pillow. Shelly giggled, put her ring finger right in front of Nicole's face, and shook her hard while she screamed, "Nicole! Wake up! I'm getting married in two days! Come on, Nicole, wake up!"

Nicole slowly opened her eyes but shot to her feet when she noticed the ring on Shelly's hand. She grabbed Shelly's hand, looked at the ring, rubbed her eyes, looked at the ring again, and started squealing. "I'm not dreaming! It's real! Yes! It's about time you two got engaged. I was beginning to wonder if it would ever happen! Oh, Shell! I'm so happy for you! And, Curly, you did a good job. It's a beautiful ring. So, when's the date? Have you talked about that yet?"

Shelly giggled, blushed, and looked at Curly before telling her of their plans. After more squealing and giggling, Nicole got very serious all of a sudden and shouted, "What! That means just two days to plan a wedding! Someone get me some paper and a pen. We've got a lot of planning to do and need to start making lists." Nicole started hunting around the cabin's desk for some paper but was distracted by a sleepy voice saying, "Hey, could y'all hold it down? How's a kid gonna git some sleep with this racket?" Tucker rolled over and sat up in his bed while rubbing his eyes. "What's goin' on anyways? Someone else git killed?"

"Umm...no, Tucker, no one else is dead that we know of. Listen, your mom and I have a question for ya. How do you feel about having a dad in two days? Tonight I asked Shelly to marry me, and surprisingly she said yes." Curly reached out and tried to straighten Tucker's hair that was standing up all over his head.

"Seriously? You mean I'm getting a new mama and a new pa all in one week? Wow! That's totally cool, man! Yeah, I'd be okay with you as my dad, but you'd better treat Miss, I mean, Mama Shelly good, or you're in for a heap of trouble."

Curly chuckled as he pulled him into a hug before answering, "No problems there, son. I happen to love her quite a bit. Now it's about eight minutes to midnight, so we'd better head down to the security office. Remember, everyone needs to look upset until we're behind closed doors. We need to convince people that Tim's in big trouble. Let's go."

A few minutes later, they were sharing their news with Tim and Officer Ortega. After all the congratulations were over, Officer Ortega cleared his throat and said, "I hate to be the one to stop this party, but we still have a murderer on the loose and only have two days to catch him, and I have no suspects. Now I'm going to place Mr. Beaufort into a fake house arrest, which means that he'll be escorted to his cabin and a guard will be placed at his door. Meanwhile, I have to find someone else who's connected to all three of our victims."

The officer put Tim back into handcuffs before leading him back to his cabin with the rest of the group somberly trailing behind. Once at the cabin, he instructed one of his men to stand guard and told Tim that he would have to stay in the cabin. Pulling Nicole down with him, Tim sat down on the couch once the officer departed.

"Well, if I have to be locked in my cabin, I must say that I'm glad that I have such a beautiful woman to share it with me. Listen, y'all, I'm totally exhausted. I'm thrilled for you two, but I'm going to have to send you on your way so that we can get some rest.

Shelly, why don't you give Nicole a call midmorning so that you two can start the wedding plans?"

"Sure, night, you two." Shelly agreed as she and Tucker followed Curly into the hallway. Once the door was shut, Curly loudly said, "You two go on to your cabin and get some sleep. I'm going to see if I can convince Officer Ortega that someone other than Tim has done this. Night." Curly winked while placing a quick kiss on Shelly's forehead and watched as Shelly and Tucker went to the elevator that would take them to their suite. *I'm such a blessed man. Lord, thank you for giving me Shelly. Would you please show me or Officer Ortega what we're missing so that we could wrap this case up tonight? I'd like to spend my wedding day with no worries.*

Chapter 22

Curly entered the security office to discover Ortega sitting at a long wooden table with files and papers strewn haphazardly all over it. Curly cleared his throat, and Ortega looked up. "Oh! You startled me. It's been so quiet down here this evening. I am glad that you came back tonight. I hope you can make more sense of this than I've been able to. I've been studying these files since all of you left with Mr. Beaufort and haven't turned up a single usable lead. Here, take the Craddock file and let me know if you think of anything. You have my permission to look at any of these."

Curly took the offered file, pulled out one of the soft leather burgundy office chairs, and got busy reading. He spent the next half hour just rereading all the files. Once he had read all of them, he turned to Ortega and said, "We know Mrs. Craddock and Mrs. Schmidt had close relatives onboard, but I can't find any known relatives in Ramone's file, which is very brief. Do you have his employment records yet? Have you had a chance to run Ramone's name through Interpol's database?"

"I had just started looking over Ramone's employment record here on the ship's database when you entered. As far as I can tell, he has no negative reports. In fact, he's received numerous awards and letters of commendation for his service. Here, you take a look." Ortega turned the flat panel monitor so that Curly could read it.

"How did Ramone get this job? Would this database also tell us that?"

"Yes, it does. Just click on 'Employee Profile' there on the top of the screen."

After doing as instructed, a new screen opened up with Ramone's full name, address, phone numbers, passport information, emergency contacts, etc. "It states here that Ramone was hired based on a reference by Carlos Rodriguez, the ship's pharmacist. Hmm, Rodriguez is a common Hispanic name but could it be possible that it's his brother?"

"Let me see," Ortega re-positioned the monitor so that both men could read it. After skimming the information on the screen, he picked up the inner ship phone, put it on speaker phone, and spoke. "Please connect me with the pharmacy."

Curly listened as Ortega asked for Carlos and was told that he was off until nine in the morning. After Ortega disconnected the call, he looked over at Curly and asked, "What do you suggest? Should we wake the man at two in the morning or wait for a more reasonable hour?"

"Normally I'd say wait, but we're running out of time here. Why don't you send one of your men to get him? While we're waiting, we can run Ramone's name through Interpol's database. Never know what kind of history he had before working here."

"Agreed. Sounds like a good plan." Ortega picked up his radio from his desk and called one of his men to tell him to bring Carlos Rodriguez to his office. After getting that started, Ortega closed the employment records and logged into Interpol. Once on Interpol, he typed Ramone's information into the database and then sat back to wait. In just a few minutes, a report opened up that included his photo.

"Man, I'm glad you had his passport information. With a name as common as Ramone Rodriguez, we would've had to sort through hundreds of people," Curly said while skimming the report. "Oh, man, check this out. See that? Says that he was suspected of money laundering for the drug cartel, but they could never get enough evidence for an arrest." Curly sat back, raked his fingers through his hair, and whistled through his teeth. "That opens up a whole new train of thought."

"The evidence had to have been slim, or the cruise line would never have hired him."

"Sure, sure, I understand, but criminals slide through the system every day. Well, maybe Carlos will be a relative or a close friend and be able to give us some more information. While we're waiting, let's start a flowchart of each victim and what motive anyone..." Curly was interrupted from finishing when a security officer entered the office with a Hispanic man following him.

Ortega jumped to his feet and offered Carlos one
of the chairs for a seat. "Please have a seat and forgive
us for getting you out of bed at such an ungodly
hour."

As Curly watched Ortega make Carlos
comfortable, he paid attention to Carlos's attitude
and body language. *Obviously he's been in bed. Anyone
could tell that by his rumpled look. He appears to be
open with nothing to hide. Lord, I sure hope he gives
us a lead here. This case is quickly hitting a brick wall.
Please give me and Ortega the right questions to ask.*

Curly kept his own notes while listening to
Ortega confirm that Carlos was indeed related to
Ramone and that the two were cousins and not
brothers. "So, Carlos, tell us why you never came to
ask about him if you two are related," Ortega asked.

"What? Why would I come here and ask about
him? If I wanted to talk with him, I'd just go to
his cabin, man. Wait! Is Ramone in trouble or
something?" Carlos looked from one man to the
other, trying to read the men's faces.

"Oh, forgive me! I thought everyone onboard
knew by now! I'm sorry to be the one to inform you
that earlier today your cousin, Ramone Rodriguez,
was found dead. I am sorry that you had to find out
this way." Ortega spread his hands and bowed in his
head in a gesture of apology.

"Dead! No way! Not Ramone! Why would
anyone want to kill Ramone?" Carlos slammed his
fist on the table in anger and leaned toward Ortega
while demanding answers.

Ortega held his hand up before answering, "Sir, I must demand that you control yourself and sit back in your seat. I'm curious about something. I said nothing about Ramone being murdered, yet you assume he's been killed? Why do you say that he's been killed?" Ortega asked.

"Well, umm...because Ramone's the healthiest man I know and keeps himself in good shape. So, with these other people that have been killed recently, I just assumed he had been too. Did he die naturally? Is that what you are telling me?"

Ortega allowed a small grin to show and paused a full minute before continuing, "No, no, you were correct. He was poisoned. May I ask where you were all day today... oh, I mean, yesterday?"

Chapter 23

Wow, Lord! I'm getting married in just two days! It's just so hard to believe that this is all real, but this ring on my finger is sure helping! Thank you for bringing Curly into my life, Jesus. He's such a godly, honorable man—not to mention he's also so handsome with those curls all over his head! Now I have a wedding to plan that is less than forty-eight hours away! Yikes, I'm starting to panic here, Lord! How on earth am I gonna get everything finished in time? I'm going to need a dress. I guess I can look for one in Nassau. Oh my gracious! We need to ask the captain if he's willing to officiate...

Shelly eventually fell asleep while mentally going through her to-do list. Before she knew it, she was being shaken awake by Tucker. "Come on, Mama Shelly! Wake up, please!" He was pleading by the time she peeked through her eyelids at him.

Pulling a pillow over her head, she groaned, "Ugh! What time is it anyway? I feel like I just fell asleep."

"It's seven. You said to wake you by seven. Come on, we don't wanna miss a minute of Nassau."

She rolled over and patted the bed for Tucker to sit down next to her and rubbed her hand over her face trying to wake up.

"Listen, Mr. Beaufort told me to call midmorning. That's not seven in the morning. I'll probably call them around nine-thirty. So why don't you get your tablet, sit on the balcony, and play Minecraft until I'm ready to greet the real world? Maybe you'll see those dolphins."

"Okay, if I have to. Hey! How 'bout I see if I can hang out with Curly, I mean Mr. Rogers? Maybe he's tracking down clues and could use my help!"

Trying not to laugh, Shelly smiled. "Well, only if it's okay with him. Go ahead. Go knock on his door and see if he's up yet. Be sure to come tell me if you do go with him."

"All right! Yes, ma'am!" Tucker shouted as he bounded to his feet and raced to open the door. She could hear him knocking on the door and what sounded like Curly's voice. A couple of minutes later, her ship phone was ringing.

"Hello?"

"Hey there, beautiful! Guess someone wouldn't let you sleep, huh?"

"Hey, Curly. No, he's way too excited to just sit or sleep."

"Well, I just wanted to let you know that he's with me. I haven't even thought about going to bed. Ortega and I made some progress last night, but I'll fill you in later. You need to sleep. Oh, one more thing..."

"Yes?"

"The captain came by early this morning to check on Ortega and me to see if we're making any progress on this case. While he was there, I asked him about us getting married. He said that he would be honored. And he also said that they have a staff member that helps with all the details, so I hope it's okay if I set it up for her to come by your cabin at nine-thirty. Is that okay?"

"Oh, Curly! Yes, it's okay! In fact, it's more than okay. I was worrying over all of that when I should have just turned it over to the Lord and gotten some sleep."

Chuckling, Curly replied, "Well, glad I could help answer a prayer then! Her name is Miss Hortchez. Sweet dreams, beautiful. You have almost two hours before she'll be there. Love ya."

"Love you too."

Curly disconnected the phone and turned to Tucker. "Okay, partner, let's go meet Ortega at the breakfast buffet. Now listen, you have to promise me that you won't interrupt us while we're talking because we have a lot to do today."

"I promise. And, boy, am I hungry!"

The two made their way to the lavish breakfast buffet that had everything from simple continental cuisine to a full hot meal. After loading up several plates with the scrumptious food, they sat down at the table where Ortega was already eating.

"Judging by the amount of food you two have, I must assume that neither of you ate dinner yesterday evening?" Ortega asked as he bit into one of the biggest strawberries that Tucker had ever seen.

"Oh, we ate a delicious supper last night, but this all looked too good to pass up. Ortega, Tucker's going to be joining us this morning. I hope that's okay. He understands that he's to watch and not to go off on his own."

Ortega reached out his hand, shook hands with Tucker, and replied, "Perfectly fine. I believe before we went to our cabins to freshen up that we had decided to talk with Mark Craddock, Janet Schmidt, and Carlos Rodriguez again to see if we could nail down who benefits from these deaths. When we meet with them, I'm going to introduce you and then allow you to lead in the interview since I have already met with each of them at least once."

"Yes, I agree. You know, Ortega, the more I think about it, the more I'm liking Mark Craddock as our guy."

"Mark? What's your theory? Excuse me a moment, Tucker, would you please get me some more coffee? Caffeinated, please."

"From everything Tim and Nicole have said, Mark's never once acted as if he ever cared for Mitsi, his new wife. Why marry her if he didn't even like her? I believe that he needed money and took out a large life insurance policy before the wedding. He then planned on murdering her by poison and carried it onboard with him, probably disguised it as a medicine."

"But why would Mark want Barry and Ramone dead? How do those two deaths benefit him?"

"I think that he just killed those other two to try and cover the real murder up. He wants it to look like a madman is a serial killer just killing anyone."

"But if he's the killer, how did he manage to kill Barry? You watched the spa's security footage with me last night. No one matching his description went into the spa during the time Barry was there."

Curly sighed and said, "I know. We've got to be missing something. Let's go talk to these three and see if we can learn anything new. Who are we starting with?"

"I've already called and scheduled our first meeting with Janet Schmidt. Mark Craddock wasn't in his room when I called, so we'll check his cabin after meeting with Mrs. Schmidt. I figured that we could drop in on Carlos at work after we've talked with the other two."

"Sounds good. Come on, Tucker, time to show you what real police work is about. Remember, be quiet as a mouse, okay?"

"Yes, sir. You won't even know I'm there."

They followed Ortega off the elevators to the Schmidts' cabin door. As Ortega approached the door, Curly once again sent a quick plea heavenward. *Please show us something, Lord.*

Chapter 24

Curly and Tucker waited patiently while Ortega rapped quickly on the cabin door and then paused to listen for any sounds. "Mrs. Schmidt? It's Officer Ortega."

The door opened slowly, and Curly was surprised to see that Janet Schmidt was standing there dressed in a matching tennis outfit with her makeup on and hair fixed. *Hmm...I expected to find a grieving widow. This lady does not appear to be grieving about anything.*

"Mrs. Schmidt, let me introduce you to Detective Greg Rogers and his young friend, Tucker. I know you and I have already had an extensive interview, but Detective Rogers would like to ask you some additional questions." Ortega didn't wait for a reply before walking over to the couch and patting it. "Tucker, why don't you sit here beside me? Detective, you can take the desk chair, and, Mrs. Schmidt, why don't you sit on the edge of the bed? Detective, I'll turn this over to you now."

Curly watched as Janet glanced at her watch, grimaced, and walked over to the vanity. Leaning against the vanity, she said, "I prefer to stand, thank you. I hope this isn't going to take too long because I have plans this morning."

Curly took a small notebook and pen out of his shirt pocket before answering, "It shouldn't take too long. Let's get started then. Please describe your marriage with Barry."

Janet sighed, stretched, fluffed her hair, and said, "It was fine, just like I told the officer earlier. We had our tiffs, but what married couple doesn't?"

"Really? That surprises me with what we've been told regarding his temper. Usually someone with that kind of anger will take it out on his spouse and children. He never hit you or the kids? Never belittled you?"

"Well, I said we had our tiffs, didn't I? Sure, he hit me some and called me all kinds of names, but I knew he didn't mean any of it. He always felt bad about it later. Usually, it was because he had one too many beers."

"I see. How did your family feel about his treatment of you?"

Janet shrugged and laughed before responding, "My family? Yeah, right! My dear ole mom was too afraid of him to say much. And my dad left all of us when I was only two years old. Never heard from him since! My oldest brother, Jake, he's as mean as Barry was. Now my baby brother, Jeffrey? He's the gentle one in the family. He never even liked seeing a spider get killed. He saw Barry smack me once, and he begged me to leave or call the cops. But...wait! What does any of this have to do with anything?"

"Just questions we have to ask." Curly reassured her. "So where does Jeffrey live? Did he come along with you all?"

"Jeffrey? He lives in Greensboro, North Carolina, about forty minutes from our house. On this ship? No way! Last I heard, he was going hiking on the Appalachian Trail for two weeks."

Curly took a moment to jot some notes down and then looked up to see her reaction to his next question. "I understand that you and Barry were both pretty upset with Mr. Beaufort when he removed your children from your home. You were quoted as screaming, 'You'll regret this!' at him. When's the last time that you or Barry had any interaction with Mr. Beaufort?"

"Mr. Beaufort? Who's that? Oh! The social worker?" At Curly's nod, Janet waved her hand while answering, "Oh, the last time we talked with him was so long ago that I can't even remember when."

"Well, how do you feel about Mr. Beaufort? I understand you saw him onboard the ship. How did that make you feel?"

"Well, he's not my favorite person. I mean, why should he be? That man took my babies from me and for no reason whatsoever! But it's all worked out now. Until I saw him a couple of days ago, I had totally forgotten about him. How much longer is this going to take? I'm to meet my friend on the tennis courts in just a few minutes."

"Please, just a couple more questions and we'll be through for now. Did you know the waiter, Ramone Rodriguez?"

"Ramone? Isn't he the other man who was killed?" At Curly's nod of agreement, she continued,

"Yeah, I knew him. He was our waiter. We had the late dining time, and Ramone did an amazing job serving us, although Barry usually found something to complain about. It's just awful what happened to that man!"

"What about Mrs. Mitsi Craddock? Ever meet her?"

"The first person killed? Nah, well, Barry and I did see her and her husband arguing in the elevator late one night. When we heard what had happened, Barry told me he thought her husband must have done it because he didn't act like a newlywed." Janet stopped to look at her watch and exclaimed, "I'm late! I must insist that you leave now. If you have more questions, come back later, but I must go."

Curly made his apologies for making her late then led Ortega and Tucker towards the elevator. While waiting for the elevator to arrive, Curly leaned over to whisper in Tucker's ear. Tucker grinned and went off running for the stairs. Just when Ortega started to ask what was happening, the elevator arrived and they stepped inside. Curly was thankful for the solitude so they could talk openly. "Anything strike you as odd during that interview, Ortega?"

"Not really, other than our newly widowed Mrs. Schmidt not acting like she's very upset over her husband's death."

"Yeah, I agree. Too bad her brother isn't on board. The gentle brother, what's his name?" Curly thumbed through his notes until he found the name,

"Oh yes, Jeffrey. Now, he might have a motive if he were on this ship."

Ortega sighed and said, "Another suspect. Just great! Let me check the ship's computer and make sure he isn't onboard. Excuse me for asking, but what did you say to Tucker to get him so excited?"

Curly laughed and answered as they exited the elevator to make their way to the Craddock's cabin. "Just an idea I'm checking. Mrs. Schmidt was really eager to not miss her tennis appointment and was dressed up really nice. By nice I mean makeup on, hair fixed, etcetera. Don't know too many women who get all fixed up just to exercise, so I started wondering who this lady is meeting. Maybe she's got herself a boyfriend. Tucker's been wanting to help me with this case, so I asked him to go get an ice cream cone from the station close to the tennis courts. While getting the cone, he's going to pay attention to whom she's playing tennis with. Since he's a kid, she'll never even notice him."

"Ahh, that's quick thinking, Rogers. Well, here we are at the Craddocks' cabin. Let's see if he's back by now.

Chapter 25

Man, I finally get to help Curly out! Man! This is so totally cool! I can't wait to tell my buddies back home about this! Maybe I'll be the one to "crack the case" for them like Brittany did when Mama Shelly was kidnapped. At least, Mrs. Schmidt is easy to spot with that tennis getup she's wearin'.

Tucker wanted to appear casual as he strolled down the deck toward the tennis courts, so he decided to make himself a chocolate ice cream cone at the ice cream station. He took a cone from the dispenser and slowly pulled the lever for the chocolate ice cream side. Just when he thought he was close to making the perfect cone, it slipped off into the collection tray. *Ugh! This isn't as easy as I thought it was gonna be!* He bit his lip as he gave it another attempt. The second try didn't come close to looking like the cones from his ice cream shop back home, but at least, this time it stayed on the cone. He quickly started licking since the high temperature was making it melt all over his hand, and he turned to start watching Mrs. Schmidt play tennis. Fully expecting to see her on the court, he was dismayed to discover the courts were empty. *No way! She was just there! Man! How could I be so stupid? Think, Tucker, where could she be at? Oh, man! What am I gonna do? Curly was countin' on me, and I lost her all 'cause of a dumb ice cream cone!*

He threw the cone into a trash can and slumped down onto a nearby bench. Just as he was getting ready to admit defeat and head back to the cabin to find Curly, he saw Mrs. Schmidt and some guy come around the corner. Mrs. Schmidt was laughing and giggling at whatever the guy was telling her. Tucker pulled out his notebook and started jotting notes down just like he had seen Curly do.

Mrs. Schmidt with some tall blond dude.

Tall blond dude has arm around Mrs. Schmidt's shoulders'.

The couple finally got their rackets from their bags that were on one of the lounge chairs and walked right in front of Tucker as he started playing with a rubber band he had found in his pocket. As they passed by, he overheard Mrs. Schmidt saying, "Oh, Stevie! You're so sweet to me..." He didn't get to hear the rest of it, but he had enough for a new entry.

Tall blond dudes name is Steve.

Watching the couple begin playing tennis, Tucker quickly grew bored watching her act as if she had never held a racket before in her life. Every time it was her turn to serve, she would call Stevie over to show her what to do. *She'd learn more quickly if she'd quit giggling at him every single time he shows her something. Girls are so dumb! I think 1 have time to make another cone.* This time he didn't try to make the perfect cone and just made one as quickly as he could. When he finished, he was relieved to see that they were still playing and hadn't left.

Again, he sat down and started licking as fast as he could while looking around at all the different kinds of people walking around on the deck until he heard Mrs. Schmidt call out, "Oh, Stevie! Let's stop now! I've run so much I feel like a limp noodle!"

"Sure! What would you like to do next? Go off the ship to the port?"

"Well, I would rather go see that show they have today in the auditorium this afternoon. Barry would never take me to any of the shows, and I would really love to see one of them. But before I do that, I need to take a shower!"

"Sounds good to me. Let me walk you to your cabin, and then we'll meet up at the show."

Tucker decided that he'd better head back to his own cabin and not try following them again. He chose to take the stairs instead of waiting on the slow-moving elevator and quickly jogged up them and to his cabin. As he was unlocking the cabin door, he could hear voices from inside.

"Oh, good! Curly, you're here! Wait till you hear what I got! Hold up a minute! I thought you were going with that Ortega dude to talk to Mr. Craddock. Why are you here?"

Curly sighed as he wiped his mouth. "Mr. Craddock refused to talk to us. He said that he's already told us all that he knows, so I decided to stop and eat a quick bite before going to talk with Rodriguez's cousin. And I definitely wanted to see

Shell a little bit while I was eating. So, tell me what you found."

Tucker pulled out his notepad and showed it to Curly as he excitedly jabbered away, "She's already got a new guy, and her husband hasn't been dead a coupla days! Doesn't look like she misses her Mr. Schmidt, does it? The whole time she was, like, 'Oh, Stevie!' and fluttering those eyelashes and giggling the whole time! It was disgusting! Hey! Can I eat lunch now too?" Tucker asked Shelly as she came from the bathroom, putting on her watch.

"No, Tucker, you're going with Nicole and me into port. We're going to grab something quick to eat there, and then we're doing some serious wedding shopping. In fact, I'm glad you came back when you did because I was just getting ready to come looking for you. You ready to go?" she asked as she grabbed their IDs.

"Ugh! Shopping? I mean, I'm glad that you're gettin' married, but how come I have to go shoppin'? Can't I just keep helping Curly?"

Curly bit back a smile and replied before Shelly had a chance, "Now, Tucker, these two ladies need a man to escort them. I really need for you to go with them. That would be a much bigger help for me right now. Okay?"

Tucker rolled his eyes, sighed, and said, "Yes, sir. Sure, whatever. Can I, at least, pick where we eat lunch?"

Shelly laughed as she ruffled his carrot-colored hair. "That's a deal as long as I don't see any more eye rolling or bad attitudes. How about this? If we get our shopping done and you have a good attitude about it all, I'll plan on taking you to the waterslide when we get back."

"Okay! Let's go. Come on! What's taking you two so long?" Tucker raced to the door and held it for the two ladies as he tried to rush them out of the cabin. "I bet we can find your dress in under an hour!"

Shelly looked at Nicole and Curly and shrugged while saying, "We're coming! Bye, Curly. Be careful, and remember, I'm praying you figure this out today! Love ya!"

"Love ya too, hon!" Curly replied as he watched the door shut behind his soon-to-be wife. He put his head in his hands and prayed for wisdom before going to find Officer Ortega. *Lord, please watch over those three today, and please, I'm begging here, please show me the way to the solution of this case.*

Chapter 26

Shelly, Nicole, and Tucker were pleasantly surprised at how quickly they were able to make it through the ship's security before leaving the ship. They figured that most of the people had disembarked during the early morning hours, so they were able to move right through since it was late morning. Once they had made it through customs at the port, they started walking down the local street looking for a place to eat. Tucker immediately spotted the golden arches of McDonald's just after they had walked a few blocks.

"McDonald's! Yes, my favorite! That's what I'm picking for my lunch choice!" Tucker shouted as he skipped ahead, kicking small rocks off the sidewalk.

"Seriously, Tucker? McDonald's? You are in another country! Why don't you look for a grill or small cafe that is Bahamian so we can try something new?" Shelly suggested as Nicole agreed.

"Nope! Umm, I mean, no, ma'am. I don't like trying nothing new."

"Tucker, what have I told you about your grammar? Please say that correctly."

"Huh? Oh, I meant to say, 'I don't like trying anything new.'"

By that time, the trio had arrived at the front of the McDonald's, which didn't have indoor seating. It was set up more like an ice cream shop in the States. They got in line, ordered, and sat down at one of the picnic tables that was set up under the shade of a giant palm tree. After they had thanked the Lord for their food, Shelly looked at Nicole and said, "Listen, I feel awful about dragging you along with me when you should be spending the day with Tim. You are on a honeymoon, you know."

Nicole shrugged as she replied, "Some honeymoon! More like a nightmare! Don't worry about it. There's no way I'd let you buy your wedding dress without my expert advice! Not only that, but Tim and I've already discussed going away for a long weekend in the next month or so since this cruise has been ruined. So, don't worry about us. Tim and I are thrilled for you and Curly."

"Nicole, how are you really doing? This is me you're talking to—your best friend. You doing okay or are you feeling like you're going under?"

"Oh, Shell, right this minute? I'm okay, but I'll be the first to admit that I'm so scared that my stomach has been hurting nonstop since they started suspecting Tim. That's why I'm just eating a milkshake for my lunch 'cause my stomach is in knots, which is a total bummer when our cruise has such awesome food, and I can't even enjoy that! I know that Curly wouldn't lie to us, but I keep thinking that maybe his arrest is real and not a fake. I just keep trying to remind myself that none of this has taken God by surprise. Every time I start feeling overwhelmed, I just remind myself to cast my care back on Jesus's strong shoulders like Peter tells us to do in first Peter."

"Good for you! You're doing great! And don't forget that you're not alone. Curly and I aren't the only ones praying for you. You have a whole school and church back home praying on your behalf. Just one piece of advice—remember, this can either make your marriage stronger or totally ruin it. It's all in how you and Tim communicate and handle it. Okay, that's enough heavy stuff. Let's start talking about some fun stuff. My meeting with the ship's wedding coordinator was awesome! I've decided to use one of their bouquets—it's beautiful! The flowers, and no, I have no idea what kind of flowers they are. You know how bad I am with that. All I can tell you is they are light lavender and pale pink, so we'll want to find you a dress that has either of those colors in it. They're also going to take care of the pictures, wedding cake, music, and setting up a video uplink for my family in Ohio."

"Excuse me, Mama Shelly, may I be finished?" Tucker interrupted, growing tired of the wedding talk.

"Yes, you may, especially since you ate all of it! Throw away our trash, would you, please? And I brought your tablet since you are so addicted to Minecraft. That will keep you occupied while Nicole and I finish planning." As soon as he had gotten involved in his game, she continued, "Now, where was I? Oh, so the only things we need are a dress and shoes for me and you because the fellas all brought formal wear for the ship's formal meal. That is, if you want to buy a dress."

Nicole laughed. "Not want to buy a dress? Are you nuts? We might be in the middle of a murder investigation where my husband is a person of interest, but this is still me, you know! I'd really love to, but I promised Tim that I'd hold the spending down in case we still need to hire an attorney."

"Well, Curly thought you'd feel that way, so he gave me his credit card and told me to get you one as long as we agree to be reasonable. I told him that we agreed! He really wants me to enjoy my day, and he knows that means having fun with you shopping."

As Nicole started squealing, a native Bahamian man approached their table and sat in one of the empty seats without being invited. He leaned in close to Shelly and said, "Pardon the interruption, but I would like to show you our beautiful city. For only ten American dollars, I can give you a wonderful walking tour and include in the tour a stop at a lovely banyan tree that is only a five-minute walk from here."

"Cool! Let's do it, Mama Shelly! That's an awesome price!" Tucker said, losing all interest in his game.

"Tucker, please. No thank you, sir. Now if you'll excuse us." Shelly started to pick up their belongings but was interrupted again.

"Ah, but, Miss, I promise you that you'd have a lovely day." The man persisted as he pulled a cigarette-looking item out of his pocket and started rolling it between his thumb and first finger.

"I've already given you our answer. Now please leave before I start yelling for police at the top of my lungs." She waited until the man had walked out of sight before speaking again. "Sheesh! The nerve of some people! Just because we don't have a man along with us he thought we'd fall for that! Yeah, a walking tour! Somehow I have a feeling that we wouldn't have had a tour! Well, let's get us a taxi and head to that shop the coordinator told me about."

On the ride to the store on the other side of town, Shelly and Nicole had to answer Tucker's many questions about what had just taken place. He had really believed the man, and they had to convince him that the man was trying to trick them. He finally started asking about the cigarette. "Is that what cigarettes in the Bahamas look like? That one he was rolling between his fingers? 'Cause it didn't look like one, I mean, any that I've seen at home."

Shelly paused before answering, "I really don't know, Tucker. Do you, Nicole?"

Nicole raised her eyebrows and answered, "Umm, yeah. We've seen similar ones at our other stops. It's what they call a joint, Shell."

Shelly then took advantage of the moment to give Tucker a reminder about marijuana's devastating effects and how it or any drugs could wreck and ruin a person's life. She was still going strong when the taxi came to a stop in front of a quaint but upscale ladies' boutique. She stopped midsentence to pay the taxi driver, so Tucker took advantage and quickly started playing on his tablet before she could continue. When they exited the taxi, they took a moment to look around at how different the stores were than in the United States. Everything looked so much run-down than back home.

Once they entered the store, Tucker chose to sit in one of the chairs by the front window and continue playing his game while they shopped. After they had been trying on dresses for over an hour, Tucker grew tired of his game and started watching the people walking by on the sidewalk outside.

Sure, there are some different kinds of people who live here. Every kid I've seen has been barefoot with hardly any clothes on. Hey! Wait a minute! That looks like Mr. Craddock walking down the street! Wonder why he's here on the same street as us. I'd better go tell Mama Shelly.

Chapter 27

Curly met up with Ortega and made their way to the ship's pharmacy to see if they could get anything new out of Carlos. As they approached, Curly was shocked to see it full of people leaning against walls, counters, and shelves holding their sides.

"Wonder what's going on? Is it normal for the pharmacy to be this busy?" Curly turned and asked Ortega as they entered.

"No, it's usually very slow in here. Something must be going on," Ortega answered. He excused himself as he worked his way to the front counter to find a frazzled young Chinese girl helping a mom with a sick toddler. "Excuse me, Miss. I'm Security Officer Jorge Ortega. What's going on in here?"

"Oh! Hello, it seems that these people are all on this cruise for a large family reunion, and they all drank local water at our last stop. So now they're all sick. When will people understand that we're just trying to protect them when we say to not drink the local water? Well, that's not your problem. How may I help you, Officer?"

"I just need for you to call the back and ask Carlos Rodriguez to come out here? Please don't tell him that I asked."

"Sure, just a minute." The girl did as she was instructed but was shrugging in apology as she hung up. "I'm sorry, sir, but he's out to lunch. They said he's scheduled to be back at two."

"Okay, thank you. Please don't tell him that I was here. I'll get out of your way and let you get back to helping these people." Ortega walked back to the corridor and informed Curly of the news. After discussing several ideas, they decided to go find Janet Schmidt and her friend, Stevie. They went to her cabin first but weren't surprised to find it empty. They reread Tucker's crude notes and went to the auditorium hoping that they had decided to stick to their plans. The crowd was small for the magic show since the ship was in port, so it didn't take long to spot her sitting at the end of a row with a tall blonde man next to her. Ortega discreetly approached the couple and requested that they follow him. He led them to a room off the back side of the auditorium that had a sign stating, "Employees Only."

"Mrs. Schmidt, I apologize for interrupting your show, but Detective Rogers and I have a few questions. First, please introduce me to your friend here."

"His name is Steve Freemount. Couldn't this wait?"

"No, ma'am, it can't. How long have the two of you known each other?"

Both of them answered at the same time but with different answers. Janet quickly replied, "I just met him this morning," while Steve blurted out, "We went to high school together."

Curly asked Steve, "Now this is interesting. Why are you lying to us, Mrs. Schmidt?" When she didn't answer but just kept staring at him, he turned to Steve. "So, Mr. Freemount, did you come on this cruise just to meet up with Mrs. Schmidt?"

"Really! This is absurd! I must insist that you stop this nonsense. He's just a friend." Janet interrupted before Steve could answer.

"Mrs. Schmidt, please! I was asking Mr. Freemount the question. Well, Mr. Freemount?"

"It's like she just said. It's just that we're friends from high school who just bumped into each other onboard. I don't see what the big deal is," Steve replied.

"Really? Just bumped into each other, huh? You let acquaintances call you 'Stevie,' huh? So, you don't mind if I also call you that, Stevie?" Curly taunted.

"How did you know about that? Who told you? Listen, Buster, you leave her alone! She'd never hurt anyone, and if I hear that you keep harassing her, I'll—"

Curly leaned in close to Steve and interrupted. "Yeah? You'll what? Poison me too?"

"Why, you!" And before either of them could move, Steve punched Curly in the nose. "That's what I'll do! Now step out of my way!"

Ortega grabbed Steve's arm and wrenched it behind his back as he snapped handcuffs onto his wrists. "You aren't going anywhere, Mr. Freemount.

You're now under arrest for assault. Now have a seat and simmer down. I suggest you answer our questions if you want to avoid any more problems, understand? Detective Rogers, are you okay? Or should I call for the doctor?"

Curly had grabbed a towel from the cabinet and was holding in over his spurting nose. "I'll be fine. I've had worse. I'd rather just finish up here. Now, Mr. Freemount, how long have you and Mrs. Schmidt been together?"

Steve grunted, looked at a sobbing Janet, shrugged, and replied, "We befriended each other on Facebook about a year ago and started chatting. All totally harmless, just friends. She's had a rough life being married to that jerk, Barry. We grew closer online, so when she told me that they were going on this cruise, I decided to come too. We had only met up twice at the lounge before he died. World's a better place without him if you ask me, but I wasn't the one who poisoned him. If I would have killed him, I'd have used my hands! Anyways, he died while in the spa, right? Well, during that time, I was getting a golf lesson. Feel free to check it out."

"Oh, don't worry, we will." Ortega assured him. "For now, you're coming with me to the ship's holding cell. You coming too, Detective?"

"No, I'll let you handle that. Why don't you also check with the ship's golf pro and see if his alibi is solid? I'll go talk with Carlos."

"Okay, just come down to my office when you finish." Ortega led Steve down the corridor with the sobbing Janet following close behind. Curly waited for the blood to stop flowing so he could clean his face up before heading back to the pharmacy. *Great! Nothing like a black and blue face for wedding pictures! Maybe Nicole can cover it up with some of that makeup she has all over their counter!*

Curly returned to the still crowded pharmacy to discover Carlos helping the young girl at the front counter. When Carlos spotted Curly making his way through the crowd, he vaulted over the counter and started shoving people out of the way as he went sprinting down the hallway. *Lovely! Now I get to chase someone, Lord! Maybe I should've gone with Ortega!*

Chapter 28

"Tucker, please don't interrupt me when I'm talking! Nicole, I think that dress isn't quite you. The flowers on it are *huge*!" Shelly said as she turned back to the dress rack to look for a better dress.

"Mama Shelly, please! I just saw Mr. Craddock!" Tucker was so worked up trying to get Shelly's attention that he kept bouncing from one foot to the other.

"Tucker, what did I just say about...wait! What did you just say?"

Blowing out a frustrated sigh, Tucker pointed to the front window and said, "I just saw Mr. Craddock! He was walking down the other side of the street!" Tucker grabbed her hand and dragged her over the window so he could show her. "See? You can still barely see his back."

Shelly scanned the street and finally spotted Mark Craddock indeed walking on the same street where they were. *How strange! We took a taxi to this shop. How on earth did he manage to get here*? "Nicole, could you come over here, please?"

"Hey, Shell, check this dress out! I absolutely adore it, and I've already tried it on! It fits great! Do you think it costs too much?" Nicole asked while walking toward Shelly and looking at her great find.

"Yeah, it's fine. Nicole, listen, I think we might have a problem. Look out this window and down the street. That's Mark Craddock out there! Tucker noticed him a few minutes ago. See him?"

Nicole looked through the smudged glass window and saw the men talking and pointing toward the store. "Um, Shell? It might be nothing, but after all that's been going on. I'd feel better if you would give Curly a call and see what he thinks."

"Great idea!" Shelly pulled her cell phone out but was dismayed to discover that she didn't have any service. "Oh, Nicole! Duh! We're not in the States or on ship, so my phone doesn't work!"

Nicole turned to the exquisitely dressed lady sitting behind the counter and sweetly asked, "Excuse me, ma'am, but we really need to contact our friend onboard the cruise ship, and our cell phones don't work here on the island. May we please use your phone? We'd be glad to cover the charges."

The lady graciously offered the phone for their use without charging anything, and even dialed the number that went directly to Curly's cabin phone. While waiting for the call to go through, Shelly instructed Tucker to keep an eye on Mr. Craddock. When Curly's phone began ringing, the lady handed the phone over to Shelly with a reminder to keep it as short as possible.

Shelly counted six rings and was handing the cordless phone back to the store owner when she finally heard Curly say, "Hello?"

Grabbing the phone back with an apologetic shrug, Shelly shouted, "Curly! It's me, Shelly!"

"Hey, Shell! Why are you calling the cabin phone? And why are you yelling?"

"Oh! Sorry about the yelling! I'm just excited and didn't think I was going to get you. Listen, we have a bit of a development here..."

Curly listened as Shelly explained what was happening. "Shell, I don't like the sound of this at all. Some stranger tries to lure you off on a private tour, and now Mark Craddock is close by? You were right to be concerned. Since he hasn't entered the store, I believe y'all will be safe if you just stay there. I'm going to come there and get y'all. Promise me you won't leave or go outside until I arrive. Let me get the shop's name and phone number in case I need to reach you. Also, call the ship and ask for Mr. Ortega if he comes in the store or starts making you more uncomfortable." Curly jotted the information down and ended the call with a reminder to be careful.

Lord, please protect her! I hate that I didn't think there might be a problem and just sent two ladies off in a foreign country with a twelve-year-old boy! So please, I'm begging, please put a hedge of protection around all three of them! He sent his prayer to heaven as he dialed Ortega's security office. Once he had Ortega brought up to speed, he requested an officer and a vehicle.

"Craddock is there? That just doesn't make any sense to me. Why would he want to follow those ladies? I agree that you need to go meet them. I'll send Officer Franz to get a car, and he'll meet you in fifteen minutes on the pier. Call me if anything else happens. I'm still in the middle of interrogating Carlos and feel like I'm making progress, or I'd go with you."

Curly thanked him for the help and gathered his firearm, badge, passport, and key card and exited the cabin. He was fortunate to catch an elevator just as a couple was exiting one, so he was able to arrive at the pier ten minutes early. He spent ten minutes pacing, praying, and pacing some more.

Exactly fifteen minutes after hanging up with Ortega, a lime green Kia Picanto screeched to a stop next to him, and a white-blond-headed man rolled the window down and spit out quickly, "Detective Rogers, I assume? I'm Franz. Let's get a move on!"

Curly jumped in the Kia and gripped the dash as Franz plunged into the traffic by blowing his horn and screeching his tires. The street was jammed with cars, bikes, motorcycles, and people everywhere, but Franz just kept blowing the Kia's horn and working his way through the snarl.

Lord, please help us get there quickly and please keep those three safe!

Chapter 29

After disconnecting with Curly, Shelly explained to Nicole the plan and asked Tucker to keep an eye on the street and alert them if he came near the store. "Nicole, we need to waste some more time in here, so go try your dress on again so I can see it on you. While you're doing that, I'm going to go try on these last two bridal dresses and see if I fall in love with one of them."

Nicole and Shelly proceeded back to the fitting rooms that were just simple stalls divided with curtains and a privacy curtain in front of each one. They chattered about why anyone would be following them the whole time they were changing clothes and, once dressed, stepped out to show each other their dresses. "Oh, Nicole, I absolutely adore that emerald green on you, and the dress fits you perfectly! Better tell Tim to bring a napkin with him because I have a feeling he's going to drool when he sees you! So, what do you think about this one? I don't even need to try the other one on because I absolutely love this one." Shelly slowly turned so Nicole could see her dress from every direction.

Nicole grinned and whistled as she replied, "Oh, Shell, it's lovely, and so are you!

I love the way the material just floats every time you move. Curly's going to faint when he sets his eyes on you in that dress!"

As Shelly started to respond, Tucker interrupted her. "Mama Shelly! Wow! You look beautiful! But you'd best change right quick 'cause I think I see Curly gitting out of a really bright green car, and y'all don't want 'im seein' ya!"

Shelly squealed and ran back behind the curtain, while Nicole laughed. As she was straightening her hair, she heard Curly's voice talking with Nicole and Tucker. *Thank you, Lord, I feel safer already just knowing he's here!* She pulled the privacy curtain back, left the dress in the room so Curly wouldn't see it, and joined them at the front. "Man, Curly, am I ever glad to see you!"

Curly pulled her into a hug as he replied, "Same here, although I wish I knew what's going on here. Are you okay?" He stepped back and looked her over to reassure himself that she was indeed okay.

"Yes, I'm fine. All of us are, but what are we going to do? We can't stay in this shop all day!"

"Franz and I discussed that on the way here." Seeing her perplexed expression, he explained. "Franz is one of Ortega's men, and he just dropped me off. We want to follow Mark, so we can see what they're up to. Did you finish all your shopping? Or do you have more to do?"

"We have our dresses but need to get shoes, and I'd like to find a lightweight suit for Tucker."

"Good. Franz is going to meet us at a small deli just a couple of doors down from here. We'll walk there, and I'll fill y'all in on our plan once we meet up with him. Go ahead and pay the lady for your dresses. Tucker and I will be out on the street waiting."

Shelly did as Curly had instructed and was impressed when Tucker offered to carry the bag for her. The walk to the deli only took a couple of minutes, so they were entering before she even had time to think about all that Curly had told them. The deli was extremely dingy and small and was crowded with people everywhere, but the smell of fresh bread baking was heavenly. She watched as Curly stepped up to the counter and placed an order for a black coffee, two diet cokes, and a pineapple juice. As he was paying the cashier, Shelly observed a very blonde man walk up next to him. The man placed his hands on the counter, looked around, and left. After he left, Shelly saw Curly pick up and read a piece of paper that the man had left on the counter.

"Curly, what's going on? Was that..."

Curly turned and interrupted her before she could finish. "What are you talking about? I thought you and Nicole were getting us a table. Go ahead and get us one, okay?" He slowly winked at her and nodded as he realized she comprehended what he was doing.

She and Nicole went and sat at the table the man had just vacated and used napkins to clean up the crumbs and spills that were all over it. Curly and Tucker approached with the drinks, and after he was seated, he leaned in close to the ladies and whispered, "Yes, that was Franz. That note said that he spotted Mark still walking on the street, so he didn't want them to see us together. He's going to go out and stroll along the sidewalk and act like he's window shopping. In just a couple of minutes, we're going to walk on down the street to a department store. Try to act normal...laughing and teasing each other like usual. Meanwhile, he's going to see what Marcus does. If you find your purchases there, we'll head on back to the ship via taxi so he can follow them in his Kia."

Shelly and Nicole nodded and looked at each other, while Tucker started asking Curly endless questions about tailing someone. They finished their drinks and proceeded to do as planned. On the way to the store, Curly had to keep reminding Tucker to quit turning around looking for the men. Once in the store, Curly and Tucker went to look for a suit while the two ladies tried on shoes. Neither of the ladies had any trouble selecting the heels they wanted to go with their dresses, and had even paid already before Curly came looking for them.

"Wow! I can't believe you two are already finished! That has to be a world record for y'all!"

"Haha! Very funny, Curly. Normally you'd have to drag Nicole out of here after an hour or two, but both of us are more than ready to just get back to the ship. Were you able to find a suit?"

"No, but I did find a nice tie and dress shirt to go along with his khaki dress slacks that he wore to dinner last night. I'm fine with him not wearing a suit if that's okay with you?"

"Definitely! Did he tell you Nicole was wearing emerald green? Because that shirt matches beautifully!"

"Um, well, um, I actually looked at her dress to match it, but I didn't even peek at yours. I promise! Okay then, I'll pay for his stuff, and we'll get a taxi."

Curly completed the transaction and led the group to the street to hail their ride. As he was looking for one, Franz pulled to a screeching stop next to them. "Sir, I was just coming to get you and the ladies. Please get in. Mrs. Beaufort is needed back on the ship immediately. She has an urgent phone call."

Chapter 30

"An urgent phone call? Who is it from, Franz? What's going on?" Nicole demanded as Franz quickly drove the Kia in and out of the congested streets.

Franz shrugged as he looked over at her before pushing his hand down on the horn to encourage a group of women to quit talking and to get off the street. "I am sorry, Mrs. Beaufort. The captain did not tell me. He just said that I am to get you back to the ship as soon as I can, so hold on. This time of day, the streets are crazy here. It's going to take my most creative driving skills to get us through it. But have no fear, Franz will get you there!"

As he continued blowing the horn and yelling at other drivers, Nicole could feel Shelly's hand rubbing her back. "Oh, Shell! What now? A phone call? That just *has* to be about Dad! Oh, I hope he's okay. We should never have left him!"

"Shh, Nicole, let's not get all worked up before we know what's going on. I agree, it is scaring me as well, but let's just wait until we know before we get upset. Curly, why don't you lead us in prayer for whatever is going on?"

"I agree. Let's join hands and pray for Nicole and Tim." After making sure Tucker knew they were praying, the friends spent the remainder of the bouncy ride back to the ship taking turns praying for the solution to the murder cases and for the surprise call waiting on them.

Franz shouted as Tucker was starting his turn praying, "Hold tight! We're here!" As they opened their eyes, Franz slid the Kia into place right next to the ship's port. As soon as the car was stationary, Curly grabbed Shelly's hand and all the packages, instructed Tucker to grab Nicole's hand, and shouted, "Stay together but walk quickly!" After the harried long walk back up the port, they were all breathless as they approached the ship's security entrance. "Shell, it looks like they're waiting on us. I see the captain and Ortega. I'm as curious as you and Nicole. What could be going on?" Once they cleared the security checkpoint, the captain immediately approached Nicole with a bland look on his very tan face.

"Mrs. Beaufort, please follow me. This steward will be happy to carry any packages you have back to your cabin."

"Oh, yes, thank you! But please! Please tell me what's happening and why Franz was in such a hurry to get us back?"

"Just follow me, I would rather we talk once we are in the privacy of my office." The captain then led them through a door labeled, "Off Limits," and they found themselves being led through a hallway they had never seen before, which was obviously for staff since it was not decorated. Due to using the staff corridor, they were able to reach his office in just a few minutes without encountering any crowds. When he unlocked and opened his door for her, she was relieved to see her husband, who ran to her with open arms. As she received the much-needed comfort, she demanded again, "Now, what's going on?"

"Mr. and Mrs. Beaufort, I apologize for the secrecy and the delay in answering you, but truthfully I am in the dark as much as you are. Please use my phone to return the call. All I have been told is that it is imperative that you return this message as soon as possible. Here is the message that was given to my assistant, along with the number that you are to call. Again, use my phone as long as you need to, and if you need any further assistance, please notify the steward."

Grateful for Tim's arm around her supporting her, she started dialing the number that had the area code for their hometown but wasn't a number that she recognized. "Oh, Tim! Look! This message says that it was the Clines who called. Remember them? That's the family who is keeping Dad for us. Ugh! I hope he's okay!" With her fingers trembling, she quickly punched in the remaining numbers and waited for the connection to go through. Thankfully, there was only one ring before the other end was picked up by Debbie Cline herself. "Oh, Debbie! It's Nicole Sheldon, no, I mean Nicole Beaufort. I just now got your message. What's wrong? Is Dad okay?"

"Nicole, I am so sorry that I had to call you, especially while you are on your honeymoon," Debbie breathlessly replied.

"Oh, it's quite all right. Please just tell me what is going on!"

"Well, honey, I feel so bad about this. We ate supper earlier, and your dad ate a really good meal and was having a good day mentally. You know what I mean?"

"Yes, yes! Please just tell me!"

"Well, he went to take his evening shower, so I went to clean up the kitchen. Richard, my husband, had left to go to a deacons' meeting at the church, so it was just me and your daddy. I finished cleaning up the kitchen and went to ask your father if he wanted some ice cream or coffee, and oh, honey, I am so sorry but he was gone!"

"Gone? What do you mean gone? Where did he go? I don't understand." Hearing Nicole's words, Tim gripped her other hand and squeezed to show his support.

Debbie sighed very quietly and then answered, "Honey, I have looked everywhere, but it's like he has just disappeared! I've already alerted the police, and they've put out a silver alert for him. An officer is standing right here waiting to ask you some questions, but, Nicole, before I give him the phone, I just want you to know how sorry I am. I just feel awful about this!"

"Oh, Debbie! Please don't! It's all part of that wicked Alzheimer's, and it could've just as easily been me instead of you! I am sure that they will find him soon. Go ahead and put the officer on."

After hearing what Nicole said, Shelly gasped and grabbed Curly's hand. *Oh, Lord, no! Don't they have enough trouble going on in their lives right now? Why this? Please lead them to Mr. Sheldon quickly. Have someone spot him soon before he gets hurt or sick. And please give Nicole the strength that she needs to deal with this on top of everything else!*

Chapter 31

"All right, people! Hold it down, please!" The police lieutenant tapped the microphone, straightened his belt, paused, and then resumed talking once he could be heard. "We have spoken with Mr. Sheldon's daughter, who, as most of you know, is on her honeymoon. Since it will be at least a day before she can even start to travel home, she is hoping we'll be calling with good news before she has to leave. She did tell me to express her appreciation to all of you for helping with the search today.

"Now Mr. Sheldon has been away from his caregiver for over two hours. He wandered away right after supper, so we don't have much time before it gets dark. Thankfully, it is summer, and we have a couple more hours before that happens. Since he has Alzheimer's, it is imperative that we find him quickly. Remember, those with this disease do not have their full mental faculties and will often act like a small child in their thinking process. I remind you of this because there is really no telling where he might be and why. If you find him, please call the hotline immediately. While waiting for an officer to arrive, please just sit and chat with him. Last time his caregiver saw him, he was dressed in dark blue jeans with a tan belt, dark green pullover polo shirt, lime green socks with alligator emblems, and white tennis shoes. We also have printed flyers and will give each searcher a stack to take out with them so they can be passed out while looking. Are there any questions?"

After listening to the lieutenant's announcement, Shelly's neighbor, Brittany, found herself crying, thinking of Mr. Sheldon wandering around or hurt. *Now stop crying, girl! Remember what Miss Shelly is always saying, "Don't waste time worrying—give it to God and get moving!" So I best just do that. Jesus, please lead someone to Mr. Sheldon very soon and also please keep him safe. It would be awful for Nicole to have her honeymoon ruined with her father being hurt or sick. In Jesus's name, I pray. Amen. Okay, time to go get me a stack of those flyers and get busy looking. I would love to be the one to find him!* "Hey, Mom, is it okay if I ride my bike with some of those flyers and help look for him?"

"Well, I guess that'll be okay with me as long as you promise me you'll text me every thirty minutes to let me know where you are. But please don't go in any questionable neighborhoods," Brittany's mother answered as she wiped the tears off Brittany's cheeks.

"Cool! And I promise I'll text ya! I hope we find him fast!" Brittany yelled over her shoulder as she ran to the exit to get her stack of flyers. She impatiently waited her turn by texting all of her friends and telling them what was going on. It was finally her turn, and an elderly woman handed her a clipboard for her to sign her name that she was volunteering and then handed her a stack of flyers and wished her luck. After thanking her, Brittany ran to her bright orange ten- speed and hopped on. *Okay, Jesus, lead the way!*

Brittany remembered how Mr. Sheldon always had a newspaper in his hands whenever she was visiting Shelly and he was over, so she decided to go to the library and ask if anyone had seen him today. She pedaled quickly and rode the four blocks over while trying to look in all directions at once, hoping to see him if he was out walking. She rode straight up to the door, let her bike fall over, ran into the library straight to the checkout counter, and breathlessly yelled out, "Ma'am, I need your help!" to the librarian, who was slowly putting stickers on a stack of new books.

Raising her eyebrows and sniffing loudly, the librarian responded with a harsh rebuke, "Young lady! That is no way for you to act in a library. Please keep your voice down and patiently wait your turn!"

Brittany gulped before getting the courage to go on in a whisper. "I'm so sorry, but I'm helping the police and some friends look for an elderly man, Mr. Joe Sheldon, who's missing. He's been missing for over two hours and has Alz... um... Alzhi...uh... that disease that makes old people lose their minds. There's a silver alert out for him and everything! Would you please look at this flyer to see if you remember seeing him here today?" Brittany placed the flyer on the counter and pointed at it while she continued, "He just loves to read newspapers and do crossword puzzles. I'm sure he woulda came here if he was anywhere near here."

Slowly the librarian put her stickers down and walked over to look at what Brittany was pointing at. "Well, bless his heart! He sure was in here about an hour or so ago and fell asleep over by those magazines. A young fella didn't get his way and started hollering loud, so that woke your Mr. Sheldon up. I saw him go toward the restrooms, but then someone needed help locating a book, so I really don't know where he went." Putting her hand up to her throat, she continued, "That poor man! That poor, poor man! I wish I'd have known when he was here because I would have called the police to come get him while he was sleeping. If you want, I'll keep this flyer and ask everyone who comes in to keep an eye out for him."

"That would be awesome! I need to run and keep looking, but thank you so much!" Brittany turned and ran back outside to her bike but stopped to text her mom and the hotline with what she had found out. Once on her bike, she took a moment to look around. *Now if it was that pesky Jordan that I babysit, what would catch his attention? Where would he go? Hmm, just boring houses in all directions. Wait! There's that diner at the end of this one street. Maybe he went there next!* Just as she started out of the parking lot, she got a reply text from her mother: "The lieutenant said 2 tell u 'Good job!' He's sending police over there to the area of the library."

Smiling at how she had been the one to find out something, she headed to the diner all the way looking for a white-haired confused grandpa but not seeing anyone anywhere. She arrived at the empty diner, Sam's Snack Shack, opened the door, and yelled out, "Hello? Is anyone here?" to the empty room.

"What do you want, girl? I'm a busy man and don't have no time for any foolishness or to be paying for some stupid school fundraiser."

"Oh no, sir, nothing at all like that..." She once again explained what she was doing there.

"Now that's just terrible. Your Mr. Sheldon, Joe, was a regular customer of mine, along with his sweet missus for over ten years. They came in here every Saturday for breakfast unless one of them was sick, but ever since she died and he got this awful Alzheimer's, I only see him when his daughter can bring him in for supper usually about once a month or so. But I ain't seen him at all today. Mind if I keep this here flyer? I'll show it to the supper crowd and help spread the word that he's missing. Surely someone in this small town has seen him somewhere!"

"Sure, that would be great! I gotta keep looking, but thanks again." Brittany dejectedly walked back to her bike, kicking the ground the whole way. *Great! Now where? I thought for sure that he woulda headed this way. It's already been almost another hour, and in another couple of more hours, it's gonna get dark. We just got to find him.*

Chapter 32

"Nicole, honey, I'm just waiting for dad to call me back. We're trying to find a way to get you home. The problem is that we've left Nassau and are at sea, so he's looking into having a boat meet us or something like that." Tim assured her as he held her in his arms while rubbing her back.

"But, Tim, how can I leave you? We're on our honeymoon, and on top of that, you are a murder suspect! I just can't leave you here and go home without you. Ugh! I don't know what to do. I'm so worried about dad and feel like I should be there as well. This is definitely one of those times that I wish I could be in two places at one time." Nicole sobbed as she held on to Tim even tighter.

"Shh. It's going to be just fine. Listen to me, I love you so very much, and that is never going to change no matter where you are. And as to the honeymoon part, ha! That was pretty much blown when they started suspecting me. We are definitely going to have another honeymoon once we get home and life settles down. I don't want you to worry one more second about me, okay? I do wish that I could go home with you and help you look for your dad, but Ortega can't let me while I'm a suspect. And, honey, you do need to be at home helping them look for Dad. You know, part of the reason I fell in love with you was because of the way you honor him and take such good care of him. And you never know, maybe all our worrying is in vain, and God will lead the searchers to him before you can even leave the ship! Why don't we pray again for him, okay?"

Tim started to lead them in prayer, and just as he began pleading with God to keep Mr. Sheldon safe, he was interrupted by the cabin phone ringing. "Maybe it's the lieutenant back home with some good news already," he suggested as he picked it up to answer. "Hello?"

"Tim, it's Curly. I just wanted to keep y'all up to date with any news I get from back home. My lieutenant just called, and you remember Brittany, Shelly's young neighbor friend who helped us that time Shelly was kidnapped?" After waiting for Tim's grunt of agreement, he continued, "Seems she's a smart little cookie, although we already knew that. She's been helping in the search and went to the library first. Lieutenant Marco said that she remembered Mr. Sheldon always reading newspapers and doing crossword puzzles. Anyway, the librarian said that she saw Mr. Sheldon a little over an hour ago, but unfortunately, she didn't see him leave. She told Lieutenant Marco that he seemed to be in good health and that he even got in a good nap while there. How's Nicole holding up? This has to be hard on her being so far away from home."

"She's worried sick, but this news will definitely cheer her up!"

"Well, let her know that Shelly is heading her way to help in any way she can. Tucker and I are going to do some more investigating. In fact, Ortega and I have an appointment set up to interview Carlos. After that little stunt he pulled at the pharmacy yesterday, Ortega decided to lock him up overnight and cool off. I'm hoping he gives us something that will break this case wide open. Well, I need to get going. Give Nicole my love and tell her to hang in there because all of Pilotview is out looking for him and won't stop until he's found."

"Will do. Thanks so much, Curly." Tim turned and filled Nicole in on the news. Just as he finished and she started squealing, there was a knock at the door. Tim opened it to find a very worried-looking Shelly standing there. "Come on in. I'll let Nicole tell you why she's squealing so loud." Tim stepped aside to let her in while he got out of their way by going out to the balcony.

"Oh, Shell! Brittany is officially my favorite kid right now! She discovered that Dad had been at the library over an hour or so ago. He is still missing, though, but, at least, I know he was safe and unhurt just a little bit ago. I just don't know how much more of this I can take, though. Tim's a murder suspect, Dad's missing, you are getting married..."

"Just hush, Nicole! I'm the least of your worries. Curly and I've already discussed this. We are going to give it until the morning, and then we'll decide if we're going through with the wedding tomorrow or not. I have to have my best buddy there to support me, and I insist that she have no dark clouds over her head worrying her. Curly totally agrees too."

"No, Shell! You can't postpone your wedding because of me!"

"I can and I will. What is a few days? You are much more important to me than that. Now I think we're going to see God do something awesome in the next few hours, so let's not worry about it until the morning, okay? Did Curly tell you that he's got an interview set up with Carlos?"

"Yes..."

"Well, let's start bombarding heaven so he can get a lead, clue, or something from it so we can get Tim off that suspect list and able to go home with you."

While waiting for the elevator to take him to Ortega's office, Curly kept trying to figure out what would've caused Carlos to run off like he had the day before. *I'm so glad I was able to catch him fairly quickly, but there was nothing in our first interview to indicate he has anything to hide. Only thing I recall is that they are cousins and that he helped Ramone get a job on here. Ugh! There is something I'm missing, I just know it! I feel like I've seen or read something that would point me in the right direction, but for the life of me I can't put my finger on it. Lord, please help!*

The empty elevator finally arrived, and Curly quickly made his way to Ortega's office. Stepping in the office door, he found Ortega and Carlos sitting at a card table drinking coffee. "Wow! Nice treatment for your prisoner, Ortega. I would've had him in restraints after that little stunt yesterday."

"Let's just say that Carlos and I have reached an understanding. We're going to forget about that little stunt as long as he cooperates and talks with us today. Isn't that right, Carlos?" Ortega looked sternly over at Carlos as he waited for his reply.

"Ya, whatever, man," Carlos grunted out as he slouched even further down in his chair.

"Okay, that sounds good. Carlos, yesterday I came to the pharmacy just to ask you if you knew who would benefit from Ramone's death. I am still curious to know the answer to that. Do you benefit? Or does someone else?"

Carlos shrugged as he replied, "How would I know? Man, I told you, I'm just his cousin, but since I am cooperating with you, I will guess that the obvious answer would be his wife, Rosita."

"His wife, huh? Does Ramone have a lot of money to leave her?"

"What? I have no idea. All I can tell you is that they live in this huge place that is really, really nice, and they also own a very nice vacation condo in Costa Rica, so I would guess that she is going to get something from his death. But she isn't even on this ship, so don't go thinking it's her that killed him!"

Curly held up his hand to calm Carlos down as he continued, "Calm down, man! Nobody has said anything about her killing him. Why would you even say that? Do you know something that you need to tell us?"

"No! Absolutely not! It's just that Rosita is a very sweet, beautiful woman, and I don't want to see you hounding her like you have me. She's my family, and it's my job to protect her."

"Ortega, I'm thinking we need to search Carlos's cabin since he's acting so 'protective' and since he pulled that little running stunt on me yesterday. What do you think?"

Carlos jumped to his feet and kicked over his chair. "What? Absolutely not! You can't just search my room!

Clearing his throat, Ortega raised his voice and sternly answered, "We most certainly can. Check your employee contract if you doubt me. Now sit down and be quiet, or I will put you in cuffs."

After staring at Ortega for a few minutes, Carlos grudgingly leaned over, picked up the chair, and threw his body into it. "Man! This just sucks!"

"It 'sucks' for Ramone even more. I am leaving my officer here to make sure you behave, and he will cuff you at the first sign of a problem, understand?" Ortega leaned in close to make his point while he waited for his answer.

"Yeah, yeah!" Throwing his hands up, he continued, "I said I would cooperate, and I am, so you best not go back on your word."

"Certainly not. Detective Rogers, please follow me."

Chapter 33

Standing with her hands on her hips, Brittany turned a complete circle, thinking as hard as she could while trying to guess where Mr. Sheldon might have gone. As she started to feel that it was too overwhelming for her to figure out, she noticed a young kid riding a bright red skateboard down the sidewalk.

"Hey! Can I ask you somethin'?" Brittany yelled out and was thrilled to see she had gotten his attention when he stopped and picked up the board. Running over to him, she continued, "I'm tryin' to help a friend who's lost her dad. He's this really old guy and isn't feeling too good. Have you seen any old guys wearing a green shirt out walking? Here, this is what he looks like." Brittany held the flyer up for him to see.

"That dude is lost? Girl, I just saw 'im 'bout twenty minutes ago, just a coupla streets over."

"Really? Oh yes! Finally! That is so awesome! I sure wish you had talked to 'im so I knew where he was headin'."

"Well, I did notice that he was walking toward Pilotview Central Park. When I saw 'im, he was in front of those Meadowland Apartments walkin' towards the park. But that was a while ago, there's no tellin' where he is now."

Squealing, Brittany shouted as she ran back to her bike, "Thank you, thank you, thank you! By the way, what's yer name?"

"Ben Robertson! I hope ya find 'im!"

Brittany quickly texted in the great news, hopped on her ten-speed, and pedaled as fast as she could. *Thank you, Jesus! Please keep him safe and make him stay in one spot till we find him, please!* It took her about ten minutes to bike over to the road that had the apartments on it but wasn't surprised when she didn't see him still there. She was glad to see a couple of police cars already in the area slowly cruising, looking for him as well. *Yes! They must've gotten my text! We've got to be close!*

She decided to go in the same direction that Ben had said Mr. Sheldon was walking, and before she knew it, she was at the park. Figuring he might be remembering the war he served in, she went to veterans' memorial first. As always, when she saw it, she was in awe at the huge fountain with all the names engraved on pavers around it. Just thinking about all those people who died fighting for America usually made her sad, but today she was too focused on looking for a man in a green shirt and was disappointed when he wasn't there. She decided that he had to be at the playground watching the little toddlers playing because isn't that what grandpas love to do? But when she got to the playground, there was only one family there, and they hadn't seen him at all.

Maybe he's gone fishing! I know he loves to tell me fishing stories all the time!

She raced over to the park's fishing pond but only found a couple of teenage boys throwing stones into it. They assured her that they hadn't seen any old guys walking around the pond. Trying not to get discouraged, she decided to ride the whole two-mile walking trail. *Whew! I hope he isn't still walking 'cause it sure is hot out here today, and he'll be wiped out for sure!* Many young families and couples were out taking their evening stroll, so she stopped each one of them, but no one had seen him. Half an hour later, she was back at the beginning of the path and starting to get really worried that he was walking in one of the wooded areas. Then she remembered that she had seen several kids' teams playing soccer as she was going around the trail.

Praying for direction, she started going from field to field, riding slowly by each set of bleachers and asking anyone she could if they had seen him. Every single soccer field was a dead end, but then she heard the crack of a bat hitting a ball, along with a cheering crowd! *Duh! The baseball fields! He loves baseball and is always talking about how he can't wait for Winston-Salem's new baseball stadium to be finished so Nicole can take him to a game! He's got to be there!*

Brittany found herself holding her breath as she raced over to the first field and had to remind herself to breathe. She groaned out loud when she saw that there were four different games being played. *Ugh! The lemonade that guy has looks really good. I'm so thirsty. I would stop and get one, but I feel like I'm really, really close now! Britt! Quit daydreaming and focus, girl!*

The first field was the T-ball league game, so Brittany kept getting distracted by how cute the little ones were as they tried to hit the ball, but she didn't see him anywhere, and no one else had either. She took a moment to look at the other three games going on and noticed that one of them had a huge crowd of people and was a high school league game. *I'm gonna try that one next. It would look the most exciting to him for sure!*

Taking a moment to reply to her mom's text, she assured her that she was okay and would text home when it got dark so they could come pick her up. *Dark! We've only got an hour till dark! Jesus, please help me!*

She pedaled even faster over to the big game and decided to leave her bike so she could get a better look since there was such a huge crowd. As she was looking, she continually showed the flyer to everyone she could, but no one had seen him. She walked over to the other team's bleachers and went through the whole process again, but this time a lady holding a small baby in her arms said, "Why, yes! He was sitting right in front of me just five minutes ago. He was enjoying looking at my baby. He said something 'bout getting a hot dog, but they don't sell hot dogs here, so I don't know what he meant. He is a really sweet man but a bit confused."

"Just five minutes ago? Really? Oh, wow! Where's the concession stand at?"

"Why, over that way behind the other field, but they don't sell hot dogs," the lady answered as she switched the baby to her shoulder so she could point.

"That's okay, and thanks! Hey, if he comes back, would you please try to keep him here and call nine-one-one? There are a bunch of people out looking for him. There's even a silver alert going."

"Oh no! I will certainly do that if he comes back, honey, I promise! And I do hope he's over there."

Brittany ran off as fast as she could to the concessions and about passed out when she saw him waiting in the long line. *Oh, thank you, Jesus, thank you!*

Chapter 34

"Detective Rogers, my men and I can handle this search since it is getting late. After all, this is your last night to enjoy our most delicious dinner meals. I also believe you would like to spend some time with your friends and your fiancée." Ortega started gathering up the case file photos and papers as he continued, "I am quite confident that this search really isn't necessary since Carlos has been an employee in fine standing with our cruise line for over a year now." He motioned for Curly to follow him into the corridor before locking the door and assigning an officer to stand guard.

Running his hands over his short brown curls, Curly sighed. "As much as I would love to do just that, I just can't. There will be no wedding tomorrow if this hasn't been wrapped up, so I would rather just keep going until we have the murderer in custody. I do need to check on the status of Nicole's dad and would like to grab a couple of slices of that delicious pizza y'all serve on the top deck. How about we meet back here at your office in, say, thirty minutes? It's eight ten now, so let's say eight forty-five? Will that work for you?"

After Ortega agreed to wait for him, Curly headed to Tim and Nicole's cabin. *Lord, I hope my people back home have found Mr. Sheldon by now. It's going to be dark in just a little while, and I don't want to think what could happen to him out there wandering alone in the dark. Tim and Nicole love you, Lord, and they could really use some good news.* Just as he was stepping into the elevator that would take him to Tim and Nicole's deck, he saw Tucker getting off the other one. "Tucker, what are you doing here?" He let the elevator go without him and turned to see what was going on. "Where's Shelly?"

"Hey, Curly! Cool! I was jest comin' to find ya! You are not never gonna believe this! A cop from yer office back home just called Mrs. Shel...I mean Mrs. Beaufort. And guess what? Brittany found her pa! Ain't that awesome?"

Reaching over and tousling Tucker's red hair as he gave him a shoulder hug, Curly whooped a huge, "Yes'!" just as the elevator doors opened again. Ignoring the strange looks people gave them, they got on and high-fived and celebrated from there to the cabin to find the others also rejoicing in Nicole's good news.

"Curly! Isn't God good? I just hung up from talking with both Dad and Debbie! She said that when Brittany started talking to him, he thought she was me!" Sighing and shaking her head, Nicole continued, "And on top of that, he thought he was in Winston-Salem at their new stadium watching the Dash play! He was perfectly okay other than the confusion. As glad as I am that he's safe, now I need to figure out what I'm going to do with him. How can I continue teaching if he's going to wander off like this? And he's not going into any nursing home, so y'all just don't even go there!"

Curly smiled and said, "Well, I think you should just quit worrying and relax. God is helping you and watching over him for sure! And earlier today, I went online in Ortega's office and printed off this information for you. I heard about this program a couple of months ago while at a training seminar. I think it might be just what you are looking for." He handed her the papers and turned to Shelly and Tucker. "Hey, you two! I only have a few more minutes before I have to meet up with Ortega. Want to walk with me so I can grab a slice of pizza? I'm not sure I'm even going to make it back to my cabin tonight, let alone get to see you again before tomorrow."

"Sure! Nicole, why don't you get some rest, okay? Call me if you need anything, and I'll be right here. We've got a very busy day tomorrow, so we all need to just turn in and get some sleep. Let's go, Curly. Come on, Tucker, and don't forget your tablet."

After they had left, Nicole turned to Tim and showed him the papers Curly had handed her. "Has he talked with you about any of this?"

Shrugging, Tim replied, "No, it's the first I've heard of it. Let me see what program he's talking about." As soon as he started reading, he said, "Oh! I've heard of this at my office. Why didn't I think of this for your dad? Nicole, the police have this program where they give elderly people with dementia or Alzheimer's a bracelet that has a GPS chip embedded in it. No one can remove the bracelet unless they have a special key that comes with it. Then if your father were to ever wander off again, all the police have to do is track his signal. It's a perfect solution!"

"I bet! It sounds expensive, though. I'm sure it's more than we could afford."

"Actually, it's not. We would have to purchase a bracelet, but that's under a hundred bucks. The town pays for the rest of the program. It saves them money because it is very expensive when they have to launch a full manhunt every time an elderly person wanders off. This way, they just turn on their receiver and locate the bracelet and the person wearing it!"

"It sounds wonderful, but I just don't know right now, Tim. There's so much going on that I honestly can't even think straight."

"I understand. Why don't we just keep these papers and look over them again once we are at home? We don't need to make a decision tonight. Come here." Pulling her into a hug, he continued, "I'm so glad your dad's okay partly for selfish reasons. Now you don't have to leave. I'm sure you are as exhausted as I am with this stress. I say that you go get ready for bed while I make a quick call to Dad to let him know that we won't need to fly you home. Then we are both going to bed for some much-needed rest."

***

Promptly at eight forty-five, Curly met up with Ortega, who led him to the employees' deck on the ship. *Oh! That's why deck four doesn't show up on the ship's map. I should've known!* Using his master key card, Ortega opened the door and groaned. "What's wrong? Don't tell me there's another dead body in there!" Curly stepped through the doorway to discover what had Ortega so upset. Carlos's room looked like a hurricane had blown through it. "Oh, good grief! What is this guy? A teenager? Look at all this! This is going to take us most of the night to go through!"

Sighing as he put on his latex gloves, Ortega agreed. "Yes, but remember I offered to let you sleep."

"Ugh! Now I'm wishing I had taken you up on that offer. This guy is a total slob! But standing here complaining isn't going to get the job done. Please hand me a pair of those gloves. I hope you brought a good supply of evidence bags with you."

"Yes, yes, of course. We have plenty. Let us be methodical about this. Why don't you start with his closet, and I'll take the dressers? If you see anything, speak up so I can photograph it. Once I do that, I will tag it as evidence and put it in a bag. Good luck!"

"Yeah, good luck is right. Ugh!"

Sheesh, Lord, I hope this isn't a total waste of our time. Please keep me alert and don't let me miss anything in this dump!

Chapter 35

"Honey, it's past midnight! What on earth are you doing up? You need to be asleep!" Brittany's mom reminded her when she found Brittany in their kitchen scooping her favorite chocolate and peanut butter ice cream into a huge bowl.

"Aw, Mom! I'm still too excited to be sleepin'. I really did try, but I just kepta seein' Mr. Sheldon's face when I found him. Did I tell you he called ME Nicole? Mom, what was up with that? He's known me since forever, and I don't look nothin' like Miss Shel...I mean Mrs. Beaufort!" Brittany closed the freezer door, plopped down on the bar stool, and began stirring the ice cream to get it to melt.

Sighing, her mom came around the corner and wrapped her arms around Brittany from behind. Putting her chin on Brittany's head, she carefully replied, "Honey, he's a very, very sick man. Alzheimer's disease has to be one of the hardest diseases to watch a loved one deal with. I remember when Joe, Mr. Sheldon, taught our adult Sunday school class. The other adult teachers got a bit upset because everyone wanted to go to his class because he has such a great way of explaining the Bible. And wow, could he recite verses! I never could figure out how he knew so many. No matter what your question, he knew not only which book of the Bible to go to but also the chapter and verse!" Sitting down on the stool next to Brittany, she shook her head while she continued, "I can't even imagine how difficult this is on Nicole seeing her once brilliant father reduced to the mind of a toddler at times. I've even seen him have trouble finding the book of John in church."

"But, Mom, I thought doctors had pills to cure everything. Why doesn't she just take him to the doctor and get a pill or somethin'?"

"Unfortunately, doctors don't have all the answers and cures, baby, only the great physician, Jesus, can heal all things. They're still trying to understand Alzheimer's and who is at risk for developing it. They *have* come out with a couple of medicines that can help, but they aren't a cure. Nicole did try those, but they gave him really awful side effects, so she decided to stop them. You need to understand that Mr. Sheldon is going to get a lot worse. Eventually, he won't even remember how to walk or to eat."

"Oh, Mama! That's jest awful! I wish there was something I could do to help Miss Sheld—" With a smack to her head, Brittany corrected herself. "Ugh! I meant Mrs. Beaufort! I wish I could help Mrs. Beaufort. But I'm jest thirteen. They don't need a junior high kid's help."

"Can I just say that you make me so very proud to be your mother? You are always so sweet and helpful. Let me think...I have an idea! Once Tim

and Nicole return from their honeymoon, I'll talk
to her about the possibility of you going over every
afternoon after school to 'grandpa sit.' Does that
sound like something you would want to do?"

"Would I? Well, duh! Of course! But I would
need someone to tell me how to 'grandpa sit.'"

Laughing at her daughter while putting the dirty
dishes in the sink for the morning, she replied, "It's
not that hard. Basically, you would just hang out with
him and make sure he stays at home. We'll discuss
this more tomorrow after I've talked it over with your
father. Now come on, it is time for both of us to get
in bed. I'll even tuck you in."

***

Curly slammed the closet door in frustration
and let out a disgusted groan. "Nothing, Ortega! Just
uniforms and casual clothes. Not one single clue. I'm
beginning to think we're wasting our time. Have you
found anything?"

Ortega continued searching the socks in the
drawer he was inspecting as he answered, "Sorry,
Curly, same thing here, but do not give up hope yet.
There is still quite a bit of searching for both of us to
do tonight." He paused in his search to sweep his arm
out to indicate the rest of the cabin. "Maybe in all of
this mess is the key to this whole puzzle."

Rubbing his face and sighing, Curly said, "I
certainly am praying that God points it out to me
because with all of this chaos, it's going to be easy

to overlook even a giant clue. Well, no use griping. Where would you like me to search next? The desk?"

At Ortega's nod of agreement, Curly carefully took two steps over to the desk trying his best to not step on anything, but since the floor was covered with debris, that was a wasted effort, so he decided to just step on the dirty clothes. *At least, we remembered to cover our shoes so I shouldn't be disturbing any evidence. I hope!* Before touching a single item on the desk, he used Ortega's camera to take several photos of the desktop and the contents of each drawer. Once completed with that task, he started moving the typical desk clutter out of the way so he could start skimming through all the papers strewn underneath. *This dude saves everything! There are receipts here for anything he's bought this whole year. There's even one for breath mints. Sheesh!* Deciding that a receipt could very well be useful, he began dividing the paper clutter into piles. He made one pile of receipts, one for mail, and one for just plain junk. When he finished, he realized that Carlos's mail was mostly junk and bills with just a couple of personal letters that were unfortunately in Spanish. "Hey, Ortega! Can you read these?"

Ortega took the letters and began silently skimming them. As he did that, Curly decided to see what Carlos had been up to online. Moving his thumb over the thumb mouse on the laptop, he brought the screen to life but quickly realized it was password- protected. "Have you seen anything that could be his password?"

Ortega just shook his head as he continued to read the letters. *Maybe the password will be in the drawers. Most people are foolish and write it down somewhere.* He began with the top drawer but quickly moved on when he realized it was just rubber bands, pushpins, and other office odds and ends. After giving the rest of the drawers a quick look through, he realized that he just needed to focus on the bottom two drawers, which were jammed with everything from photographs to high school awards to journals. *Journals? Bingo! Now we're talking!*

Chapter 36

Dad was right once again! I should've taken Spanish in high school. I really wish I could read these, but I'll just have to wait for Ortega to figure them out. Stacking the journals up for Ortega to examine, Curly proceeded to make a list of all the awards and photos in the drawer.

"Ortega, look! Isn't that Carlos with Ramone? And I wonder who that lady is. Oh, look! Ramone has his arm around her, so it must be his wife, Rosa. No, that's not right. Let me think...Rosita! Wow, look at the anger spilling off Carlos's face. He is literally seething with rage! This is not your happy family portrait. Rosita looks very uncomfortable as well."

"Are there any other photographs of Ramone, our victim?" Ortega asked as he picked up the first journal and sat down on the end of the bed to begin reading.

Flipping through the rest of the stack of pictures, Curly answered, "Mostly pictures from all the places he's traveled to while working on this ship. There's a couple of a sickly dog and actually a few more of Rosita, but no more of Ramone, sorry. Maybe Ramone didn't care to have his picture taken."

"Please be sure to take any with Ramone, Rosita, or Carlos in them. Oh my, now this is certainly interesting."

"What is?" Curly asked as he put the pictures into a clean evidence bag, labeled it, and sealed it.

"This journal. It appears that our Carlos is quite the writer. The oldest journal starts with his late school days. I believe you Americans call it high school." At Curly's nod, he continued, "In those, he mostly just tells what he ate and wore, but in this journal, he is writing about getting hired to work onboard this ship. He keeps referring to R. Maybe R is Ramone—no, that doesn't make sense because Ramone had already worked for us for two years. Let me skim the one before this and see if he mentions this R person again."

While Ortega busied himself searching through the rest of the journals, Curly turned his attention to the bathroom. *Nothing out of the expected here— razor, shaving cream, latex gloves, toothbrush, toothpaste, hairbrush, deodorant, and shampoo. Just the typical guy's toiletries. Wait a minute!*

"Curly! What is that word I heard you using earlier? Bingo? Well, bingo! I found it! About six months before he was hired by us, he had been engaged to this R. But then a man he calls Tablero."

"I'm sorry, Ortega, but I can only say hello and good-bye in Spanish. I don't know what that means."

"Oh, excuse me, Tablero or Rat is the name he gives this man. This Tablero 'stole her away' from Carlos, and then she became pregnant. R broke off the engagement and married the Tablero. Carlos says here that he will never rest until he has done everything in his power to rid this world of the Tablero and then make R his wife. Wow, I would say that Carlos is a very angry man. Surely all that anger could lead a man to murder, do you agree?"

"I say it sounds like we need to have us another chat with Carlos. Time is running out, and I only have a few more hours before daylight to clear Tim's name, so let's get a move on and go motivate Carlos to tell us who this Rat or Tablero is." Curly locked the door behind Ortega, and then they quickly removed their gloves and shoe coverings before half-running to the elevators. As they made their way through the back hallways to the security office, Curly started to see how all the murders were connected. "Ortega, I think I'm onto something. May I lead the questioning?"

"Certainly! I am glad one of us has some understanding in all of this mess." Ortega briefly spoke to the guard then threw open the door to the cabin they had turned into their interrogation room. At the sight of a shirtless Carlos, he froze and frigidly demanded, "Sir! Please put your uniform shirt back

"Man, it's hot in here. You've kept me waiting for hours with just a cup of coffee and a burger. I think I'm done with all of this. I'm out of here!" Carlos reached over for his shirt and stood to leave.

Oh yes! That was the confirmation I needed! Thank you, Lord! He looked over at Ortega, waiting for his signal to begin. Ortega pushed a chair over to Curly while pointing at Carlos's seat and ordering, "Be seated! You most certainly do not have permission to leave us quite yet. I have given Detective Rogers here the authority to question you. The captain and I expect you to cooperate, but please note that you do have the right to remain silent, and if you so choose to waive your right to remain silent, it could be used against you in a court of law. If you are unable to pay for an attorney, the captain will find one for you. Do you understand?" As Carlos took his seat and nodded, Ortega turned to Curly and spoke again. "Detective Rogers, you may ask anything you wish. Please just give me a moment to start the recorder and to get my notes out."

As soon as Ortega pushed the record button, Curly began. "We just finished searching that pigsty you live in. You sure could learn to clean up after yourself, but that's not a crime, is it?" Curly stretched out his legs to the side of the table, leaned back in his chair, and laced his fingers behind his head. Without even waiting for a reply, he continued, "No, it's certainly not a crime. However, we did find some mighty interesting information in there. My friend here read a very juicy story that would make a great romance for women all over the world. A story about how you were engaged to a beautiful woman, but you allowed another man to steal her away from you."

Carlos surged to his feet and slammed his fists against the table as he bellowed, "You had no right! That is my personal writings! How dare you? No right at all!"

"Carlos, I wasn't finished with the story. I suggest you take your seat and behave. Mr. Ortega has already informed you that the captain is expecting you to cooperate. Throwing a temper tantrum is not cooperating. You do that again and you'll be cuffed and shackled quicker than you can blink. Now sit down!" Curly stared at him and waited for him to obey. After a couple of tense minutes of staring, Carlos grudgingly threw himself down into the chair and pasted a sneer of contempt on his face.

"Go ahead, Mr. Smart Detective Man. You think you know everything? You don't know nothing about me. Nothing! So, go ahead. This should be quite amusing."

"You're exactly right. At first, we didn't know what it all meant because you only referred to your woman as R and to the man who stole her as Tablero, so I just have to thank you for already clearing that up for us and telling everything we needed. We now know *you* are the killer, and again thanks to you. We now know why as well."

Carlos jumped up again and jabbed his finger in Curly's face while screaming, "I didn't tell you *nothing*, man! You are lying and setting me up!"

Curly shook his head, chuckled, and looked at Ortega while replying, "I tried to warn him, but he just wouldn't listen!"

Chapter 37

"Nicole, just look at this mess! This looks worse than our college dorm room always looked, and that's saying something. There's no way I'll be able to get dressed for a wedding in the midst of this chaos!"

Shelly started organizing all the wedding clothes, decorations, and flowers that were strewn all over the cabin but stopped when she realized that Nicole hadn't answered her but was just staring out of the balcony window into the dark night. Setting the flowers down that she had been sorting, she walked over and put her arm around her best friend's shoulder. "Nicole, honey? You okay? Maybe we should just go on to bed and get some sleep. This mess can wait. I know you've just got to be exhausted."

Nicole wiped her eyes and put her forehead against Shelly's shoulder as she replied, "Yeah, I'm definitely to the exhausted level, but I just can't sleep. Every time I lie down, my mind just refuses to shut down, and I keep seeing Tim behind bars." She walked over to the bridal bouquet and started fluffing it as she continued, "Honestly, Shell? This has to be one of the hardest weeks that I've ever lived through. I don't even want to think about what I would've done if you and Curly hadn't come to our rescue."

"Oh, please! How could I resist a tropical vacation with my best friend and my handsome boyfriend? Oops! I mean fiancé! Nicole, just because you are married doesn't mean that I've quit being your best friend. We've always had each other's backs, and that is just going to keep on happening. Plus, now I get to have a wedding at sea tomorrow and become Mrs. Greg Rogers! I just realized Tucker and Tim are still gone. I thought they were just going to get some ice cream?"

"Oh, Tim told me that he was going to also see how the investigation is going. He's trying so hard not to worry, but it's getting really hard when there's just a few more hours..." Before she could finish her sentence, they heard an alarm go off. "Wow! That's so loud it's hurting my ears! I wonder what is happening now. Come on, Shell, let's go see!" She opened the cabin door and pulled Shelly along behind her into the corridor that was starting to fill with their fellow passengers. The alarm was even louder in the hallway, so both of them covered their ears with their hands and followed the other passengers, making their way to the elevator. They kept hearing people wondering what was going on, but no one seemed to really have an answer. Some people thought it was a drill; some thought it was a fire; and some people were freaking out thinking the ship was capsizing. Because the hallway was so jammed up, they didn't make it a hundred feet before they heard Big Mike making an announcement over the loudspeakers.

"Ladies and gentlemen, may I have your attention, please? We apologize for waking you at this late hour, but the ship is in lockdown. We need everyone to go back to your cabins and lock your doors. We urge you to not open your door for anyone until the lockdown has been cancelled. I repeat, do not open your doors for anyone, not even crew members until we have cancelled this lockdown." Big Mike began repeating the announcement over and over, so the two ladies turned to head back but immediately bumped into people behind them.

"Excuse us, please!" Shelly shouted and gasped in surprise when a hand grabbed her by the elbow. Pulling away, she looked up and laughed when she realized it was Curly. "Curly! I didn't expect to see you here! What's going on? Do you know why we are in lockdown?" She shouted as he led them through the throng of people.

"What? Hold on just a minute because I can't hear you over all this racket." Shelly handed him her key card, and when he opened the door, they realized that Tim and Tucker, along with Ortega, were already inside waiting on them.

Shelly watched Curly not only lock the door but also slide the deadbolt as well. "Okay. Please explain to us what is going on," she demanded as he took his gun out and checked the clip.

"Whew! At least, I can hear you talking in here. All those people and the loud alarm were starting to give me a headache." He pushed his hands through his hair and motioned for the ladies to be seated with the others. "I don't have time to tell you all of it right now, but we've figured out who the killer is. The good news is we now know for sure that it isn't Tim. Although we already knew that, but now we can prove it." He paused as Nicole started shrieking and squealing. She ran over and gave Tim a huge hug as Curly put his hand up for their attention. "Please, I know that's wonderful news, but we now have a very serious new problem. Ortega and I were questioning Carlos earlier. We had just gotten to the point that I just knew he was going to confess, and he passed right out on the floor! We—that is, Ortega and I—asked the guard to watch him while Ortega went to get the ship's doctor and I went to find some water." Sighing, Curly stretched and wearily rubbed his face. "Well, I returned to the office first and found the guard lying on the ground with a knot on the back of his head and his gun missing and, most importantly, no Carlos. That's why the ship's in lockdown because we don't want any more casualties. Ortega and I thought he might've headed this way, so that's why we are here, but we really need to get back to the search."

The whole time Curly had been giving his update, Tucker had just stared at him with his mouth wide open in disbelief, but when he heard the word *search*, he jumped to his feet and ran over to Curly. "I wanna help! Please? I'm really good at lookin' for folks. And it's gonna be really borin' to sit in here when I could be helpin' y'all look. I helped ya with

those notes earlier this week, didn't I? Please let me!"
Tucker kept looking between Shelly and Curly, not
sure which adult would be the one on his side.

"Son, I'm sorry, but the answer is a definite no.
It's just too dangerous," Curly answered as he put his
hand on Tucker's shoulder. "Carlos is an armed and
scared killer, which is an explosive combination. We
have no idea what he's going to do once we find him.
But you know what, son? I do need your help. I need
you to stay here and be the man of the family. Do you
think you can help Tim keep Shelly and Nicole safe?"
At Tucker's nod of agreement, Curly clapped his
hands together. "Good. Ortega, we best be getting to
it then. Let's go!" He strode to the door but stopped
and turned around at the last minute. He quickly
walked over to Shelly and pulled her into a big hug
while reminding her to keep the doors locked and
bolted until he or Ortega returned.

"Of course, Curly, but please, please be careful.
I want you there with me later today saying, 'I do.'"
Curly assured her that he'd be careful and then made
his exit with Ortega. *Lord, I know those two men
are professionals, so they know what they're doing, but
that doesn't keep me from worrying about them. Please
lead them quickly to Carlos and please put a hedge of
protection about them. I really would like this to be over
with as soon as possible!*

Chapter 38

Curly was pleasantly surprised to discover that the passengers had listened to Big Mike's announcement so quickly. The hallways were so empty he felt like the ship had been deserted.

"Okay, Ortega, how do you want to do this? Personally, if it were my search, I'd have us split up so that we could cover more ground even faster, but it's your ship and your search, so just point me in the right direction."

"I have the ship's security team being called in as we speak, so I will first go instruct them to start the cabin by cabin searches. Even with my whole team, that is going to be a very time-consuming task. Once I have them started, I will proceed to the Atlantic Deck and get the dining areas and kitchens cleared as soon as possible per the captain's orders. I would like for you to search the Promenade Deck. You have a loaded gun with you, yes?" At Curly's nod, he continued, "I brought this extra radio for you to use. If you need to contact me for any reason at all, please use this. I do ask that you check in after you have secured that deck. I will then let you know where I wish you to search." Ortega showed him which channel they would be using on the handheld radio and gave him a master key so he would have access to all doors. Once he had gotten Curly started, he quickly headed to his office to get the search organized. Before he had his men begin, he had the captain change Big Mike's announcement to warn the passengers that the security officers would be conducting cabin by cabin searches.

Curly jogged to the elevator and groaned when he realized it had already been shut down. *I didn't realize they had done that already. Great! Now I've got to use the steps.* Already exhausted and knowing the night was not even close to being over, he half-jogged down two levels from the Empress Deck to the Promenade Deck. Knowing that the Promenade Deck was where the ship's stores, casinos, and lounges were, he decided to begin on the end with the stores. *Lord, this could take us hours, if not days, to complete. I'm supposed to be getting married in just seven hours. I'm begging you to please lead one of us to find Carlos quickly.*

Thankfully, each store wasn't very large, so he was able to quickly clear and secure each of them before heading to the casino area. Unfortunately, he realized he was going to have a major problem securing it since it was an open area located between the stores on one end and the lounge on the other. It felt strange to walk among the tables and not hear the usual noises of people gambling and drinking. The smell of cigarette smoke still lingered in the air, as it was the only area onboard where passengers were permitted to smoke. He quickly cleared it, and moving on to the lounge, he pulled open the wooden door separating it from the casino. He stumbled as he tripped over a stool due to the room being pitch-black. Wishing he had his flashlight from home with him, he groped the wall feeling for the light switches. After a few more stumbles, he finally located them behind the small bar area set up near the entrance door. Once he had the lights on, he was able to move quickly through the room before approaching the backstage area. *Now this is going to take some time. All these wardrobe racks, costumes, and props would make an excellent hiding place.*

Meanwhile, Ortega and his men had begun their respective searches—the men going cabin by cabin and Ortega searching the Atlantic Deck. Since that deck held the dining locations, he knew he needed to clear it quickly, so the captain could give the kitchen crew permission to get back to their breakfast preparations. He started in the kitchen of the Platinum Restaurant and began methodically checking every cabinet and storage container as quickly and thoroughly as possible. Listening to his men as they checked in via their radios, he realized they had a lot of passengers that were very upset about the searches. Knowing it was necessary, he still hoped they wouldn't have to upset many more and that Carlos would be quickly found.

"Ortega, this is Detective Rogers checking in as you requested. I have cleared and secured the Promenade Deck and have seen no sign of Carlos or that he has been here. Where to next? Is anyone checking the pharmacy since that's where he worked?"

"Yes, I have a couple of my men searching that area now. Please continue by going to the Lido Deck, which is deck nine."

"Copy. I'm on my way now. Also, when you or one of your men has a moment, would you please check in on Shelly and Tucker? They're okay for now. I just checked on them after clearing the Promenade Deck. I would really like it if you could put a guard on their cabin because with Carlos framing Tim for all these killings, I just don't feel too comfortable leaving them without protection."

"I understand and agree completely. Once I have finished clearing and securing this deck, I will check on them myself and stay with them until I get one of my men in place to stand guard."

"Very good. Over and out." Curly felt a measure of relief knowing that Shelly and his friends would be safe. When he stepped out onto the Lido Deck, he realized that he would only have half the deck to search since the other half was made up of suites, which Ortega's men were searching one by one. *I seriously doubt he would hide up here by the pools, but it still has to be cleared. Lord, I'm running out of patience. Please guide me, Ortega, and all his men. And please keep Shelly and Tucker, along with Nicole and Tim, safe from Carlos. Thank you!*

Chapter 39

Think, Carlos, think! Where can I hide where no one will find me on this stinking ship? I just have to make it another day and a few hours until we reach Florida, so surely there is somewhere that I can hide out and not be found. Thinking through all the different ideas he had and the pros and cons of each, he went straight to the employee laundry area and grabbed a uniform from his buddy Jaquan's locker. *Oh yes! This will work! Jaquan is close to my size, and since he is a security officer, no one will look twice at me during this ridiculous lockdown they just started.*

Hearing the announcement change from the ones he had been hearing, Carlos stopped to listen to see if they were lifting the lockdown but realized it was just instructions about the cabin searches that were beginning. Smiling, he took the time to check his appearance in the employee restroom before heading out to put his new plan into place. *Excellent! No one will even dare to question me. I just need to avoid that Detective Rogers and Mr. Ortega and I'll be a free man!* Walking carefully but quickly through the hallways, he didn't encounter anyone as he made his way to the elevators so he could head to deck seven. Already knowing exactly where the best spot to observe from was, he pushed the elevator up button and cursed when he realized it had been shut down. Knowing this meant he would have to use the staircase; he looked around, paused, and listened for any footfalls, voices, or radio chatter. Not hearing any signs of people, he quickly proceeded up to deck seven. Once there, he paused to see if the corridor was clear. Seeing someone coming on the side, he quickly strode down the corridor on the opposite side of where he had been spotted. *Drat! That's Detective Rogers! Well, it looks like he didn't see me, and it also looks like he ain't staying either. I'll just pretend like I'm headed to the suites at the very end. I still can't figure out what he meant when he said that I told him I was the killer. I never said nothing! How did I slip up? What did I do?*

Thankful that Curly had stopped to check on her and give her an update, Shelly decided to get some fresh air by sitting on the balcony. *I just love the peacefulness of the ocean at night. It's so calm, and the sky is so clear I feel like I can see all the way up into heaven!*

"Mind if we join you, Shell?" Nicole asked as she stepped through the balcony doorway.

"Oh, not at all. Come on out and enjoy the peace and quiet with me." Shelly scooted some chairs over and then continued, "Where's Tucker?"

"He's sitting on the couch watching cartoons and playing his tablet. I say he'll be sound asleep in about ten or fifteen minutes. One reason we came out here was to give him some quiet time," Tim answered as he reached over to hold Nicole's hand while stretching out his legs. "I declare it sure was good to hear I'm no longer a suspect. Curly certainly came through for us, Shell! Although I do believe I'm going to need another vacation to recuperate from this one. What do ya say, hon? Want to head to Gatlinburg after we get off this Horror Cruise?"

Sighing, Nicole replied, "Oh, that sounds absolutely lovely. But, Tim? We can't. We have Dad to take care of, remember? Unless you want to bring him with us."

Shelly interrupted the planning. "Why don't we just get through today, and once we're all okay and at home, I'm sure that the trip can be arranged. Curly and I haven't even discussed where we want to honeymoon. After how yours has turned out, I'm not too sure that I even want to go on one." They all laughed, and she started to get up at the sound of a knock on the cabin door.

"I got it, Mama Shelly!" Tucker yelled as he ran to open the door first.

"Remember, Tucker, to make sure it's Ortega or Curly... " Shelly didn't get to finish but watched from the balcony doorway as he opened the door and a security officer stepped in after saying something to him.

"It's okay, Mama Shelly, it's just a security officer. He says he's supposed to search every cabin on this level, even though I done told him that no killer would be stupid enough to hide here."

Chuckling, the officer stretched out his hand to Shelly and announced, "Ma'am, I'm Officer Lewis. Please just stay seated while I conduct a quick search.

I know this is a horrible inconvenience, but I promise it won't take long." After Shelly had sat down next to Tucker on the couch, the officer went into the bathroom and came out a few seconds later and opened the closet. "Looks like your son was right. No one is hiding in here, but you do have one big problem."

"A problem? What's that, Officer?" Shelly inquired.

"Would you kindly get your friends in here so they can also hear?" Shelly opened the door, and after explaining to Tim and Nicole, they all came in and found a seat.

Tim spoke up. "Okay, we're all here. So, what's the problem now?"

"The problem is that I am not Officer Lewis, but I am Carlos, the man that everyone is looking for." Pulling a gun from the back of his waistband and pointing it at them, he continued, "I figure no one will think to look for me in here, not in the cabin of that hotshot detective's girlfriend! Now don't get all upset because I'm not going to hurt anyone as long as you follow my instructions and stay quiet. I just need to hide out here until we reach the port, and then I'll be on my merry way. If anyone comes to this door, I want this here boy to answer it and to tell them that everything is okay and that the cabin has already been searched. Got it?" At their scared faces and nods of agreement, he pulled the desk chair over and sat down all while keeping the gun pointed right at them. "Good. That's exactly the way to follow my instructions."

Chapter 40

"Greg, Ortega here. I have been diverted to an employee's cabin. Seems we have a missing security uniform. All of my men are currently being used in the lockdown, so if you want your friends checked on, it will need to be you." Ortega ended his transmission as he made his way to the belly of the ship where the employees resided.

"What? He has a stolen security uniform? With that, he'll be able to go anywhere on this huge thing! I am going up to check on my friends. Will check in when I am there." *Lord, I don't like this one bit. Please keep everyone safe. I just want to marry Shelly and get back on dry ground!* Since everyone was in lockdown, he was able to move quickly to level seven. As he was approaching her cabin, he received a Facebook message alert on his phone. *Who on earth would be messaging me?* When he pulled out his phone to see if it was anything important, he froze in his tracks. *Oh, dear Lord, no!*

Meanwhile, back inside Shelly's cabin, Carlos had moved everyone to the couch. Since the couch wasn't long enough for all four of them, Tucker was made to sit on the floor. As Carlos kept the gun trained on them, he pulled the chair from the desk over, turned it around backward, and sat down. "Now I see four very good reasons why the captain will have to let me off here a free man. Jaquan has to be missing his uniform by now, so I expect we shall be hearing from someone here very soon. Don't do anything stupid and everyone should be fine."

Realizing the danger they were all in, Tim hesitantly spoke up. "Um, Carlos, right? I don't understand. What could I have done to you that you would have had to do all of this?"

Carlos snorted, leaned back a bit, and laughed. "Done? You specifically haven't done a thing except be in the wrong place at the wrong time. When you were the one who purchased that 'special' nausea patch you became...how do they say? Oh yes, you became my scapegoat."

As Carlos was mostly watching the adults and not paying much attention to Tucker, Tucker started frantically praying and thinking of something he could do. He realized Carlos didn't know that he still had his tablet in his hands but didn't think that would do much good. Then he had a brainstorm! He slowly slid his finger over and tapped his Facebook messenger app. His chat with Curly was the last chat he had on there, so it was the one still open, so all he had to do was press the video button while making sure anything coming in was muted. *Lord, I sure hope he gits this and that this works. We need some help bad and soon!*

Out in the hallway, Curly was frozen as he watched the scene that was taking place just a few yards away from him in her cabin. *Oh, Lord, what have I done? I was the one that told them to stay in that cabin thinking they'd be safe! Now this nut job has them! Please help us!* He quickly typed a response to Tucker, letting him know he was watching, and asked him to try to keep the video going as long as possible. When he got a thumbs-up back in response, he went back to the other end of the hallway so he could use the radio without being overheard in the cabin.

"Ortega! This is Greg. You are needed on level seven immediately."

"Greg, I am quite busy here talking to my officer, Jaquan, the one who is missing his uniform. What is it that you need?"

"Jaquan's uniform is currently being used in Shelly's cabin!" Before he could continue, Ortega broke in on his transmission.

"Copy that. Heading your way."

While waiting for Ortega, Curly continued to watch the video. It made him sick seeing Carlos so smug and confident that his plan would work. In fact, Carlos was so confident that he was enjoying telling Tim all about how he had laced the patch with poison and didn't care who died while wearing it. When Tim asked him why he would even want to kill some random person, Carlos just sneered and shrugged before replying that he only wanted to kill his cousin but knew he would be suspected, so he had come up with this "masterful" plan to hide Ramone's death in with other deaths.

At that point, Ortega rushed up to Curly and demanded, "What's this about the uniform being up here? Why are you out here in the corridor?"

Holding his finger up to get his attention, Curly turned his phone so Ortega could watch what was happening. After watching for just a few seconds, Ortega pulled his radio out and called the captain. "Sir, we have located Carlos. He is currently holding Mr. and Mrs. Beaufort, Shelly Gale, and Tucker Gale in Miss Gale's cabin. Advise how you would wish me to proceed."

"I will come to you there on deck seven. Meanwhile, start evacuating all of the others off level seven and have them taken to the Platinum Dining Room and make sure they are comfortable."

"Copy that." Ortega turned to Curly and said, "You go into your cabin and continue watching that video. Meanwhile, my men and I will start clearing this floor. When the captain is on floor, I will ask him to make your cabin our headquarters."

Curly did as Ortega commanded, being sure to turn his radio down so Carlos wouldn't be alerted to all that was going on around him. When he opened the door to his cabin and saw his tux and thought about the upcoming wedding, he about broke down right there into tears. Struggling for control, he took several deep breaths and continued praying while he waited.

Chapter 41

Yes! I knew Curly would come through! I don't think this dude is going to let us live. Usually on TV, when the bad guy tells ya everything, he kills ya. I hope Curly can figure something out! Tucker carefully stretched his leg and leaned his head against Shelly's leg as he listened to Carlos telling Tim how easy it had been to sneak into the spa and just randomly pick a room with someone waiting on their masseuse. *This dude makes killing people sound like it's a big deal. I wish I was bigger. I'd just slug him one!* Since his head was on Shelly's leg already, he nudged her leg with his head so she would look down and see how he was in contact with Curly. He knew the moment she did because she started rubbing his arm up and down and giving it a squeeze in between the rubbing.

After listening to Carlos brag about sneaking into the spa, Tim was dumbfounded. He shook his head, ran his fingers through his hair, and said, "You killed two random people just to kill your cousin? What on earth could make you hate your cousin so much that you would want him dead? Whatever it was, surely it could have been worked out peacefully without people having to die!"

Carlos jumped to his feet and got in Tim's face. "Peacefully? Ramone was not an honorable man! He stole *my* woman from me! Rosita! She loved *me!* But then Ramone came along and started telling her all kinds of lies about me, and she married *him!* He is a dog! I spit on his name!" He turned and spat into the air while all four reached out and gripped each other's hands, realizing they were dealing with a madman.

While Curly watched Carlos's crazy rantings, he also kept an ear to the radio and listened as Ortega was very quickly moving all the civilians as quietly as possible off the floor to the dining room. A few minutes later, Ortega radioed that the captain would be entering his cabin shortly. At the sound of a key card, Curly stood to his feet and put his hand on his gun. When the door opened, and showed that it was indeed the captain, he relaxed. The captain reached out his hand while speaking quietly. "Detective, while I am thankful we now know who the guilty party truly is, I do regret that your friends' lives are in jeopardy. You have my word— we will do all we can to get them out of this safely."

"Thank you, sir. I do appreciate it. I believe I just heard that Ortega has cleared the last room and is heading our way. Honestly, Carlos sounds like he plans on using my friends in exchange for his freedom."

"Well, we will not allow that. Ah, here's Mr. Ortega now. Mr. Ortega, do you have a plan?" the captain demanded as he walked over to the small table, sat down, and motioned for the other two to be seated. Curly waved off the offer and replied, "Thank you, but I am too worried to be still."

Ortega sat, tipped his chair back, and closed his eyes in thought while Curly paced. "Sir, Carlos is not aware that we know he is in that cabin. My first thought is to have Greg try to open the door as he would normally do and as he was going to do anyway to check on his friends. Then we will see how Carlos responds and will then work out how to proceed from there."

The captain drummed his fingers on the table and then gave his nod of approval. Curly didn't waste a moment. He immediately went over to Shelly's cabin and attempted to open his door with the extra key she had given him and his gun in his other hand while shouting out, "Hey, y'all! Just thought I'd come check on you! What's up? How come you have the dead bolt on? Although I am glad y'all are being so cautious!" Trying to sound as normal as possible, Curly waited and then continued, "Shell? Nicole? Where are y'all? Why isn't anyone answering me?"

Inside the room, Carlos grabbed Shelly and dragged her to the door while holding the gun to her head and keeping his eyes on the others. Leaning close to her ear, he whispered, "Be very careful and say what I tell you. Tell him that I am in here and that I demand to speak to only the captain." Shelly trembled and squeaked as she followed his orders.

"Curly, hey! We're all fine. I can't undo the dead bolt because there's a guy in here by the name of Carlos. He has a gun on us and is demanding to speak to the captain."

"Carlos! Can you hear me?" Curly shouted.

"Yeah, I'm standing right here next to your beautiful lady, although she is not nearly as beautiful as my Rosita."

"Listen, I have Ortega with me. He'll have to be the one to get the captain. That's going to take a few minutes. Why don't you let the ladies and Tucker go? You'd still have Mr. Beaufort as a bargaining chip, but there's no reason to keep the ladies and child in there too."

"When I hear the captain's voice, I will agree to let the women and child free. But don't try playing any funny games, or I'll kill them all."

"Let me go see if Ortega has contacted the captain yet." Curly went back across to his cabin to confer with Ortega and the captain on how best to proceed.

Ortega looked up and asked, "Rosita? Who is Rosita? Why does that name sound familiar?"

"She's Ramone's wife but was Carlos's girl first. I knew he was our guy when he had his shirt off because he has Rosita and his name tattooed in one big heart on the left side of his chest. I just haven't had a moment to tell you before now."

"Ah! Now I understand. And good going on the negotiation. We will have the captain 'arrive' in five minutes to speak to him. We don't want him to realize we are right across the hall."

During the five minutes, the three brainstormed different ways of getting Tim out unharmed if Carlos did indeed let the women and Tucker go. At the end of the five minutes, the captain stood to his feet, strode across the hall, and rapped loudly on the door. "This is the captain. I understand you wish to speak to me. I will agree to speak with you only after you release the women and child."

They all froze as they heard the door being unbolted. Ortega gently moved the captain out of range as Tucker came flying out, followed closely behind by a tearful Shelly and sobbing Nicole. As soon as Nicole was out, Carlos slammed the door, and the sound of the dead bolt being turned was heard.

"Captain, if you want to see this man alive, I must have a helicopter and a million dollars in one hour, or he will die," Carlos said.

Chapter 42

Curly pulled the three into one big hug while assuring a distraught Nicole that they were going to do all they could to get Tim out alive.

"Tucker, that was some awfully smart thinking turning on your Facebook video. Without that, we'd be way behind by now. You'll make a fine officer one day."

Tucker's face turned as red as his hair as he replied, "Aw, shucks! Us kids at school are always taking photos and videos at school without any teachers even knowin', so I figured Carlos wouldn't have a clue, and he sure didn't! Oh, did you see I left my tablet in there on the floor for ya?"

"What? Oh, man! That's smart thinking, Tucker! I haven't even looked since I went to the door. Let's go make sure Tim's okay." They all crammed around the small table to see Tim sitting on the couch with Carlos sitting in front of him with a gun pointed at his head. With his other hand, Carlos was also checking his phone like he was waiting on a call or text. "Nicole, Tim thinks fast on his feet, right?"

"Well, yes, I guess so. But why are you asking me that?"

"I've an idea, but let me talk with Ortega and the

captain first." Curly pulled the captain and Ortega aside and held a lengthy discussion. Finally, they all came to an agreement. Curly walked over and told the others, "We've got a good plan ready. Y'all just sit tight and pray!"

First, the captain used the cabin's phone and called Carlos to inform him that a helicopter was in route with the requested amount of money. They all watched on the video as Carlos got a huge grin and checked his cell phone again.

"Looks like you might get to live, Mr. Beaufort. I was kind of hoping I'd get to kill again. Oh, well, we will see if they are just telling tales or not."

Meanwhile, the captain stayed in the cabin, while Curly and Ortega left. Shelly jumped up. "Where are they going? What's happening?"

The captain smiled and replied, "Hopefully to bring all of this nonsense to an end."

Using the master key card the captain had handed him, Curly entered the cabin to the right side of Shelly's cabin. He went in and opened the balcony door and watched the time. Meanwhile, Ortega used his own master key card and entered the cabin to the left side of her cabin. Watching the time, at the exact minute he and Ortega had agreed upon, he started shooting his gun out the balcony to the sea, praying this distraction would work.

At the sound of the gunfire, Carlos jumped to his feet and turned to see where it was coming from. Tim took advantage of the moment and did a tackle that would have done his high school football coach proud. As he landed on him, Ortega entered through the connecting door between the two cabins with his gun directed at Carlos as he told Tim, "Wonderful takedown, Mr. Beaufort. If you would be so kind as to hand me his gun. Don't even think of moving, Carlos, or you will be dead."

Tim removed the gun from Carlos's hand and gave it to Ortega. Once the gun was secure, Ortega pulled a zip tie from his pocket and secured Carlos's hands and informed him he would be in holding for the murders of three people and kidnapping until they returned to port in Florida, at which point he would be turned over to the FBI.

Hearing the cheering coming from across the hall, Tim ran over and jumped into one huge group hug. Then the others stepped aside so he could assure Nicole that he was indeed completely fine.

Nicole turned and smacked Curly on the arm. "Ouch! What was that for?"

"That's for putting a plan in place that I never would have agreed to. Why, Curly, he could've been killed!"

Curly just pulled Shelly to the side and grinned. "And that is why we didn't tell you. I happened to remember that Tim had played football and figured he would take advantage of the distraction I was providing. Hey! Not to stop the celebration or anything, but we only have a few hours to get ready for our wedding!"

At that, everyone started shrieking and babbling. While they all went crazy, the captain laughed and shook Curly's hand. "Thank you for your part in ending these murders and apprehending the responsible party. I am now going to return to my duties and release the lockdown. I also believe I will be seeing you at ten." With that, the captain winked and exited the cabin.

Chapter 43

"Okay, all you guys skedaddle. Shelly and I will meet you on the Lido Deck at the bow at ten as planned, but we have a lot to do between now and then, so get ready!" Nicole hugged and kissed Tim and then shooed everyone except Shelly out the door.

Shelly plopped down on the couch and said, "Nicole, I'm wiped out! Honestly? Curly won't mind if I show up looking like this."

"Nope. No way. No how. What kind of best friend would I be if I let you show up in jeans and a T-shirt for your wedding? You aren't getting off that easy. You'll feel better after a bath, and you get some coffee in you too. Thank goodness you had your nails done yesterday. And just think, you'll have all day tomorrow to relax since we have one last day at sea."

Shelly just sighed as she watched Nicole go start filling the Jacuzzi tub. *Thank you, Lord, for getting us through another strange and crazy adventure, and thank you for good friends.* Just as she was beginning to nod off, Nicole roused her and got her into the tub while handing her a large mug of coffee. While soaking in the tub, Shelly thought through all that had happened in the last couple of days and was just astounded

that it was all due to a man coveting another man's wife. Once again, sin leads to major consequences that affect not only the person but many others as well. Much too quickly, Nicole rapped on the door and announced that she had soaked long enough.

After she had dried off and had thrown on a button-down shirt and some pajama pants, Nicole went to work on her hair and makeup. "Nicole, where on earth are you finding all this energy? You haven't stopped moving or talking for one second!"

Laughing, Nicole replied, "I had a mug of coffee myself, and I think I'm still running on adrenaline. And I just can't do enough to thank you and Curly for coming and rescuing us. I'll sleep a week when we get home, though. You can count on that! Now I must say you look stunning." Finding a mirror, she held it up for Shelly's approval.

"Oh, wow! Nicole, you're a miracle worker. I don't even recognize myself!" Shelly carefully hugged Nicole and then changed into her wedding dress. Standing in front of the mirror, she couldn't help thinking how this was not quite how she had thought her wedding day would go but then realized it was perfect because it meant she would soon be Curly's wife. Rousing herself, she turned and saw Nicole was dressed and ready with the flowers and ring, so they used the back corridors and made their way up to the Lido Deck with just seconds to spare.

When Tucker saw her, his mouth dropped open, and he was speechless. After he finally found his voice, he sputtered, "Oh, wow, um, ya look perfect,

Mama Shelly! Curly's gonna drop plumb dead when he sees ya!"

"Can we please not use the word 'dead' anymore today? And by the way, you look pretty spiffy yourself! I just wish the rest of my family could be here with me.

"We are here!" Shelly heard all their voices shout out, and she turned to see that they had been hiding behind a partition.

Shelly's dad stepped over and said, "Honey, Tim's father was so thrilled at the help you and Curly provided Tim that he arranged to fly all of us here when Tim told him about the wedding. We even got to ride in a helicopter out to the ship. And I have to say I'm very glad because I wouldn't want to miss this day for anything!" As he pulled her into a careful hug, Shelly worked hard at not crying and messing up her makeup. Before she knew it, her mom and brothers were there hugging her as well.

"All right! Break it up! We have a wedding to start right now." Nicole bossed and put everyone into position. "Tucker, hit the music." Tucker pushed a button on his tablet, and the wedding march sounded. At that cue, Shelly walked down the rose-covered aisle to the bow of the ship to begin the best adventure of her life.

Author

LIZZY ARMENTROUT

Author Lizzy Armentrout currently resides near Winston-Salem, North Carolina. She graduated from Piedmont Baptist College with a Bachelor of Science in Elementary Education and is a middle school math teacher. She is very active in her local church music ministry and enjoys reading mysteries in her free time.

LizzyArmentrout.com